A THOUSAND SHORT LIVES

W.B. CLARK

This is a work of fiction. Names, characters, businesses, places, events and incidents are either the products of the author's imagination or used in a fictitious manner. Any resemblance to actual persons, living or dead, or actual events is purely coincidental.

Cover Art by Corry Parker

ISBN: 978-0-578-29782-8

To Shannon, who gave me color,

to Genevieve, who gave me brevity,

to Corry, who gave me air,

and to Elhrick, who gives me love,

this story was written, because of *you.*

MAPS

How can you ever comprehend,
the magnificence of your world,
when you deny your flesh and bone,
the gratitude it's owed?

The complex sinews of your soul,
ache for you to rise,
and face your greatness.

To acknowledge your wild,
your stillness,
your grace between the two.

To travel the divots,
and high peaks,
that make the maps of you.

It is there you'll discover,
carefully placed constellations,
that serve as a guide,
to become all you can be.

CONTENTS

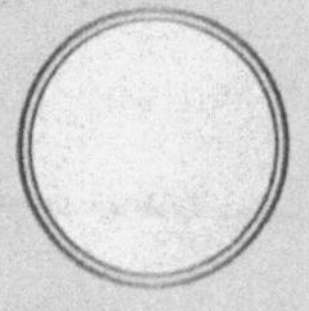

CHAPTER I

THE "KINDA" START TO AN OVERLY COMPLICATED LOVE STORY

Snow collapses from the naked branch of a tree. The clumps of white powder burst as they hit pavement, much like my dreams, much like me. I wonder for a brief second what it would be like to feel spring again, but I guess I'll never find out. My fingers twitch as I reach in a fool's attempt for my scattered textbooks and papers. *God, I know I should've waited for the walk sign, but I'm late for class. I really hate to be late…but if you could rewind time for just 10 little seconds, I'll make a better choice. I promise.*

Blood trickles from my cracked skull down into my gaping mouth; the stuff seems to be everywhere. Gathered spectators disappear as my vision darkens to black. This is really happening—I'm dying. *But why, God? Why now?*

My soul must be cursed for me to kick it this young. I was supposed to graduate with my J.D. in a few short months—with honors, too. I was really going to be something afterward. I was finally going to be happy. I was going to fall in love. I was…

.

.

.

.

.

.

.

Existing takes a heavy toll, but one forgets each time a pact is struck and the hourglass flips once more. Death is here to greet me when I am born yet again from the portal between an exhausted mother's legs. We're not exactly friends, but these quick "hellos" and "farewells" have become a joke between the two of us. Ah, who am I kidding? Death is dry as dust and never laughs. All my lovely humor is wasted on the god.

I never remember a damn thing when I'm alive…I'm

not sure if I'm thankful for that yet or not. Though I'm certain there is something important I'm forgetting when I'm in this in-between state too. No…that's not entirely right…. I'm forgetting *someone*. Their face is a blur in my long strand of memories. Why can't I see them?

A miserable scream from below distracts me from my pondering. In the ruckus, nurses try their best to force air into my shriveled human lungs while the woman who bore me keens with despair. I'm glad I don't have to be the one to tell her the last nine months have been for naught. Being human is not for the weak-hearted.

I was a boy this time, with green eyes.

. .

.

.

. .

.

.

Through the white tunnel, the harbinger of doom leads my soul to the next flesh machine for another go-round. In my new life, I'll be on a different planet at least. I know I shouldn't be judgmental, it's my journey after all, but honestly—Earth is the *worst*.

We arrive, and I ask the god for the sixty-sixth time, "Seriously though, what is the fucking *point* of all this?"

As custom, Death doesn't answer. Being my shepherd must be an extra burden dumped onto them by the Almighty, a form of divine overtime. Well boo-fucking-hoo for the dull eternal. I'd like some answers, seeing as I'm the one suffering and all. If I had physical eyes I'd roll them right about now, but instead, I observe my new body like the glowing ball of energy I am.

As far as bodies go, the two-legged creature below me is…pleasant enough. There's nothing much to be excited about—these vessels all start to rot at some point anyway. The god next to me is stiff as plywood, but even if Death is a terrible companion, I wish I could stay here with them in this in-between, where there's no hurt, no misery. But like the caked-on snow from that naked branch, it's my time to fall. On a brighter note, it's like spring where I'm going.

And

so,

here

I

go,

again.

"DID YOU...

FALL IN LOVE...

TODAY?"

CHAPTER 2

CHAOS

"Why were *you*, born?"

My lips itch to curl upward, but I do my best to keep a neutral expression. We're having a very serious conversation and I don't want Cosmos to think I'm mocking him. But oh, to be young again. To be curious about the universe and others in it.

I remember when I was that innocent; when I was little more than dust. Unlike others, I'm too impatient to even try counting how many years ago that was. I'd have to start at the beginning, and even if I do have the time for such things, I simply don't want to. It would be tedious work, and there's no point in keeping track of eternity, after all.

Across the parlor table, tea untouched, the young god waits without complaint for my answer. He's used to it by now—the waiting, that is. Cosmos has been waiting on others to notice him since the day he was spun from Venus and Mars. Though handsome enough, he blends in with the brilliance of space, his dark skin marked by a camouflage of stars.

The other gods have a cold sense of humor and pretend not to notice him. Their jest has lasted over a millennium now. This has made the youth quite lonely, but surprisingly, he has not become cruel just yet. I've known gods to throw planet-ending tantrums over smaller slights.

"*Well...*" I say slowly. I take a sip of tea and place the cup back down. This brew is entirely too bitter for my liking.

Cosmos leans forward ever-so-slightly, eager for me to continue despite patience having been beaten into him like a ruthless sea against a waiting cliff. Gods are most known for grand shows of indifference and this young one wants so very much to be like the others.

Once he realizes his impatience is showing, the constellations mapped across his skin gleam even brighter. I wonder, is this reaction his way of blushing? Cosmos averts his gaze and tucks a strand of hair, dark as the void, behind a pointed ear speckled with stars. *He truly is adorable.*

I pour more moonlight into my tea and stir the cloudy brew with a wolfram spoon, the curved edges clanking against the painted porcelain. *There*, it should be sweet enough now.

Oh yes, I almost forgot. He asked me a question about my birth. Sometimes I get carried away with all my thoughts.

"Simply put, I was born to love the darkness," I tell him at last.

His innocent eyes find mine once again, but this time, they're narrowed in confusion. "I'm afraid I don't understand."

"Do you know how old I am?"

He shrugs. "No. It's hard to tell with gods and goddesses. You could be my age for all I know. And I've found that you're not one to talk about yourself. Honestly, the universe is a large place, but you live *really* far out here. I wouldn't be surprised if the others didn't know of your existence."

The '*like me*' is left unsaid.

I found Cosmos during one of my travels inward. He was crying on one of Saturn's rings. When I asked the god what he could possibly be sad about, he stared at me in wonder, mouth gaping like a black hole. Apparently, he was shocked that I could see him. Which is preposterous—he shines with a thousand stars. I'm in tune with Evil and knew immediately of the other gods' grand-scale hoax. I couldn't bear his sweet, tear-stained face, so I extended a hand. We've been good friends ever since.

This time, I let him see a hint of a smile. "There's a reason for that. I'm charged with guarding a relic that must remain untouched."

His fingers drum against my parlor table in a contemplative manner. "You live in the middle of nowhere with hidden treasure and no one knows you? Are you by chance a dragon and not a goddess? Perhaps you've been fooling me this entire time." Cosmos is only half joking, but considering his current arrangement with the others, I don't blame him.

"If you *must* know, I'm actually one of the first gods. I'm almost as old as Time—as old as Death, even." I take another sip of my tea. *Ah*, it's just right.

His eyes widen at my revelation. "You're kidding! You're one of the Greats?"

"Mmm-hmm," I say against the cup. "When the

Almighty created the universe, I was born from one of the first stars."

"I see…you've always known your purpose, then." A shadow darkens Cosmos' happy demeanor. He's been searching his entire life for the reason why he was born, but the path for him to follow has yet to reveal itself. The god's constant worry about his value is what started this whole conversation in the first place.

I wave a hand as if I can shoo away his woes. "Heavens, no! It took hundreds of thousands of years. Like you, I started out as mere dust before I became something else."

"But what did you mean? When you said your purpose is to love the darkness?"

I sit my tea down and cradle its porcelain edges within my fingers. What I'm about to explain is challenging for young minds to understand and is usually met with rebuke. I brace myself for rejection that's surely to come.

"Every being, every act, every hateful emotion, every *sin*—deserves love. I was created to love these things, because it's difficult for others to do so. I'm the embodiment of this love, so it can exist in the souls of others."

By the way Cosmos clenches his jaw, I know I've

upset him. The young god's black eyes turn almost livid.

"You're telling me that you *love* that all the others have ignored me my entire life." He clutches his chest as if I stabbed his silver heart with my little teaspoon. "Do you know how lonely I've been all this time? How much I've suffered? And you're saying you *love* them for it?"

I reach for his star-flecked hand. "Cosmos, it's not as simple as that. Think of it this way: For every action or choice, something new grows because of it. What you consider *bad,* in this moment, will become beautiful in another. Not just for you, but for the others you'll eventually interact with. For example, we would've never met if those gods didn't ignore you, if they didn't hurt you. So *of course*, I love them. They brought me *you*. This love of mine is where the act of forgiveness originates from."

Cosmos jerks his hand away, wounded, as if my purpose has burned him. I'm not surprised. No one likes to hear that there's no good or bad, that life just simply *is.*

"What you're saying… is utter nonsense. It's… it's—"

"Chaos?" I say, providing the word he was searching for.

My friend goes rigid as he finally realizes who he's been spending his time with. I found it interesting when he didn't balk after I first introduced myself. Strange, even. For someone who's only known scorn, he's never been wary of my enigma—the god must truly possess a pure heart. Or maybe it's the naiveté of youth.

I pick up our nearly empty teacups, knowing our conversation has met its end. I'll be lucky if Cosmos ever visits me again. But I'll survive. I'm used to being alone by now, just like Time, just like Death. Solitude comes with the territory of our work. The young god doesn't look at me as I walk past; he's been here enough to show himself out.

Before I exit the parlor, I say to him over my shoulder, "The Almighty named me well. After all, I *am* Chaos."

CHAPTER 3

WHEN "WE" BECOMES "I"

A *dream* is a bountiful jungle where every leaf is a planet and every vine a road. Dying constellations become droplets of rain, and the rivers and streams are spaces that contain them. Hidden in dense shadows, always reaching for the light, are shapeshifters. These fanged creatures have the potential to mar, but are they really monsters at all, or just the fears we refuse to acknowledge? What happens if we choose to welcome their claws, instead of running away?

And what about those times when we're able to venture out into the abyss? When we're given a ship, and our sails are open to any direction, but we're not navigating tempestuous seas, no—we're in the air. *In the air*. And our hearts race because we're going somewhere different, somewhere brand new where up is down and down is up. It is here in this vertigo where we get to meet in the middle and make it our playground. And it is *here* where we're children again. Where we finally get to play.

After the joy has passed, we wake from our dream. Our eyes flutter open and we have a hazy longing to return to that special place where we can just *be*. This ache stretches on with a distance that has no end, no horizon in sight. And it is here, in this stormy prison that we discover we are truly alone, that we are no longer *we*. I wonder if I can weather these violent winds, because here I am: Awake, with nowhere to go.

CHAPTER 4

DÉJÀ VU

Two cardboard cups of steaming coffee sit between my husband and me. It's Saturday morning, and we've made a quick dash into our favorite café. He's talking to me about work, but I'm only half-listening. I'm too focused on the fact that I've done this before. But it's not the "we've been married for over a decade and snuck in a break while the twins are at soccer practice a dozen times" kind of before. No, it's more than that. This is the exact same conversation we've had, in these same two chairs, over this same table, at this same café, with the same cups of coffee.

What's even more strange, is that when I tell him, "It feels like we've done this before," his lips quirk into an amused smile, and he agrees with me.

It's déjà vu.

Later, I experience it again, a form of repeating patterns—but this time, it's in my dreams. I wake up and wonder how many times I'm going to have to fantasize about a high school crush I never confessed to. Even in the land of slumber the scene ends in failure, so why does it keep repeating?

As I hide back under the covers and pull the sheets tight to shield myself against the early morning chill, a thought to contact my old friend crosses my mind. But I know it would be a strange thing to do. We follow one another online, but we haven't spoken since graduation. Not only that, but we're also both happily married and aged well past thirty with kids. What would it accomplish? It's not like I'm still *in love* with him.

The more I think on it, I know I would look like some stalker-weirdo, the kind you see in bad films. The character who eventually gets murdered because they're fucking stupid and can't move on. I groan and roll onto my belly, face planting into the pillow. Why I am I being so *dumb*?

My husband stirs beside me, but his soft snores let me know he's still fast asleep. Down the hall, my children's bedroom door yawns as it swings open. I've got maybe five minutes of solitude until their little fists are flying and the meltdowns begin.

A list of the coming day's to-dos stacks itself behind my tired eyes. Anxiety creeps in, followed by sudden regret. Three more minutes to relish, and I turn back the sands of time. I'm fourteen again, a freshman in art class, where I first fell in love with a boy who was painting a vivid sunset, or was it a sunrise? I try hard to hold onto the creamy colors, the pinks, oranges, and yellows that remind me of gentle innocence, but my twins screaming in the distance shatters the dream.

"They're fighting over the damn TV remote this time," my husband mutters through a mouthful of morning breath.

The sheets twist around my fingers as I try to suppress all the conflicting emotions welling up inside me. I'm a bad wife, a terrible mother. How could I ever want something more, something different than what I already have? But even still, the question lingers: *What could have been?*

"DID YOU...

FALL IN LOVE...

TODAY?"

CHAPTER 5

CHAOS

I'm at the edge of the universe on a small planet whose name has been forgotten by all but the Almighty. It's a shadowy, lonesome home, but even forgotten places have gardens. I hum to myself as I trim an unruly shrub. Her velvety leaves are the color of twilight. Marta gives me the most gorgeous blooms every hundred years, and now they're just about ready. Swollen light-pink buds decorate her long supple branches.

"I'm sorry. I'm so, so, very sorry if I upset you. I'm such a fool," Cosmos' voice sounds from behind me.

I'm almost as old as Time, old as Death, and yet I can still be surprised, it seems. *He came back.*

I leave my business with Marta and turn toward the young god. He stands brilliantly in the center of my moon garden, every star on his skin shining like the miniature suns they are. Cosmos' dark eyes are earnest as they meet mine.

I tug at the fingers of my gardening gloves. "You didn't upset me. Your response was natural. I expected it."

He almost takes a step forward but then stops; his arm falls back to his side. "How can that be? You confided in me, told me your purpose and then I quickly rejected it. It's the same as if I rejected *you*. You've been so kind and yet I was cruel to you. I want to apologize properly for it."

One of my gloves falls to meet the pearlescent grass at my feet. I retrieve it as the dusty heart in my chest moves about in an odd fashion. I've never received such an apology before.

Both mine and Cosmos' hand reach for the fallen garment at the same time. This close together, the scent of his hair reminds me of forests I've traveled to in faraway places. He wins the glove, but we bump heads in the process.

"Oh! I didn't mean to do that. Sorry," he says sheepishly.

I reassure him, "No, it's quite all right."

The young god hands me the glove. Our fingers graze in the process and his stars glow brighter as he blushes. He's embarrassed again, though I'm not entirely sure why. I wish I could understand him better.

"Would you...would you like to come in for some tea?" I manage to ask.

Cosmos' smile is a warm sunrise that chases the cold night away. "There's nothing I'd like more. I've missed it."

CHAPTER 6

RESIGNATION NOTICE

I was reborn today. It wasn't an extravagant event by any means, just a simple one. So mundane, in fact, I don't think anyone else noticed. I was sitting at my desk, typing away at a report for a company that sees me as a number, not bone, flesh, and spirit, when I thought: *Fuck this job.*

And,

Just.

Like.

That.

I became something else—a new me.

I felt lighter as I packed all the drudgery away. This burden of the coveted 9 to 5 finally lifted. The want of such monotony was drilled deep into my being when I first saw my mother cry. She couldn't afford the electric bill, even though she worked so hard, most of her life accounted for in overtime shifts.

In her eyes, what I've accomplished is a dream, and she'll be upset I'm throwing it all away. But the world is different now, different from when she had to sacrifice endlessly for us. This rotating green and blue marble expanded while we all had our heads down, our noses pressed hard into infinite spreadsheets filled with someone else's data. That's the thing, it will always be ever-changing.

Just.

Like.

Me.

And,

I don't have to do *this*, anymore.

CHAPTER 7

SOUR MILK

"It smells sour, like spilled milk that's been left for too long," Callie grumbles. "You're a guy. Does your car smell like that?

"Ew, no?" I take a drag from my cigarette and attempt to blow rings of smoke into the air but fail. *Damn.* I'm not as good as I thought. I've been practicing for weeks now and had it mastered yesterday. *Figures.*

I smash the remainder of the butt against the piss-yellow brick wall Callie, and I are leaning against. It leaves a black smear of tar. When our manager sees it, he's going to flip. The thought of meticulous Greg out here with his toothbrush and soap bucket, cursing away as he attempts to make this dump of a video store shine, almost makes me smile. Almost. I squint at my coworker. "Tell him to clean his car or you won't go down on him anymore. Or better yet, stop fucking in there. You're both adults, get a room."

She rolls her doe-eyes and scoffs. "You know we can't. Not with both our living situations anyway. And a hotel would be too expensive."

I check my watch. The old face at my wrist reads 1:04 P.M., our break ended nine minutes ago. With a heavy sigh, I push off from the wall. It's time to finish the remainder of my shift. That $3.35 an hour isn't going to earn itself. I put a hand on my hip as I walk. "All I'm saying is if the car of the guy I'm banging smelled like the back of an old dairy freezer at the Piggly Wiggly, then I wouldn't be fucking him."

Callie's expression is put-out as I open the door for her. Its hinges are rusted to the point of breaking; they shriek just like my insides do when I run the register and have to listen to a customer's dumb prattle or watch them count pennies to pay for a 99-cent movie. It's always the old ladies who do it, too.

Callie grabs the return cart and makes her way to the horror section. I follow to help. Halloween was two nights ago, and customers nearly cleaned us out for some cheap thrills in front of a glowing screen. It's wild here in Texas. *Yeehaw.*

After a while, she sighs. "You wouldn't understand. You have it made and at least live by yourself. My parents would kill me if they found out. My mother has been talking with a matchmaker again. She thinks she found me someone suitable in New York." Callie sticks her tongue out, her face pinched with disgust.

By having it made, she means that my parents disowned me when they found Matt Turner and I swapping spit and other fluids in my room when we were supposed to be studying for finals. I didn't get to go to college and was homeless for a short stint, but I finally managed to get a glorious studio on the bad side of town. Its most astonishing features are the severe water damage on the ceiling and the fluorescent mold in between the shower tiles, which seems to grow back no matter how many times I scrub—I may have a scientific discovery there.

She's wrong about me living by myself, though. I have roaches for roommates. On Saturday nights, I lure them out with a miniature disco-light and they dance to a can of Raid. I don't comment on our cultural nuances. It's the South, hot as the Devil's ass crack, and both of us don't belong. At least

New York seems like it'd be a good place to live. Then again, no one is marrying *me* off. I've definitely been single for far too long if I'm jealous over something like that. On second thought, *is* there a matchmaker for gay men? It's slim pickings in these parts.

I raise a brow and hand Callie *A Nightmare on Elm Street*. "Come on. If his car smells like sour milk, how hygienic can he be in…other areas?"

Her eyes go wide at that.

The conversation between us dies down as we finally do what we're paid to do. While we restock the shelves, my mind goes to a dark place. For some reason her secret boyfriend's car really bothers me. Is it because 'Sour Milk' sounds like a shitty movie title? Since I started working here, I've become obsessed with film and it's a guilty pleasure of mine to find the worst of the worst. But deep down, I know it's not that.

I was a smart kid in school. I would've been successful if I made it to college. But I didn't get a chance, my parents' rejection took care of that. Survival came first, after all. I'm again brought back to the stench of that man's car, as if the reek coats my nostrils. It's because we're similar—my life is like a glass of spilled milk. A stain left to sour.

CHAPTER 8

WHO'S THE MONSTER?

There are two giant monsters, one pink and one blue, that rage outside the compound that used to be my everything. Now, it's shattered heaps of metal, a tomb for those who didn't escape the carnage. Over a hundred thousand lives lost in a blink because of *these* two stragglers.

Their armored tails whip back and forth, attempting to maim the other, but the only real damage they've caused has been to the last of my kind. The universe didn't succeed in wiping us out twenty years ago, so she must've sent these two to finally finish the job. I'm not surprised. My race ruined everything and now Mother Nature has come for her final recompense.

"What do we do?" Kelia pulls at my elbow, her tear-stained face is covered with soot and flecks of blood.

Our older brother didn't survive. He usually made the decisions, the hard kind that kept the three of us alive all this time. Now it's my turn, and we're most definitely fucked. I managed to get us far enough away from the gremlins, but we're like insects in comparison. They could be here in seconds if they take their fight this way.

I bite the inside of my cheek so hard it bleeds. I can't think of a plan. My thoughts are too harried, the deaths too fresh. But if I stall any longer, we'll both be dead.

"Tolly…"

I whirl on my sister. "Just give me a sec! I just need—"

But the plea dies on my tongue when I see where her shaking hand points. There in the ancient ruins, a figure cloaked in rags beckons at the two of us with a clawed hand. He's a half-breed, a *demon*. A monstrosity in every way.

"Should we go to him?"

I give Kelia a dubious stare. "You can't be serious."

The ground rumbles and we both nearly topple over from the gremlins' might. We don't have much time; they'll take their brawl this way soon.

My sister is still considered a youngster, but her

golden eyes are sharp for her years. “Do we have much of a choice?”

One of the gremlins gives a deafening roar. They’re drawing closer. I look toward the cloaked demon who waits patiently for us amidst the chaos. “I guess if I have to choose between monsters, I’ll take my chances with the smaller one.”

Kelia shrugs. “At least we won’t be crushed.”

The demon gives a razor-sharp grin. Even from this distance, he can hear us.

A sigh of defeat deflates my chest. “I wouldn’t count on it.”

"DID YOU...

FALL IN LOVE...

TODAY?"

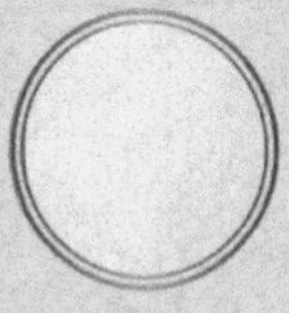

CHAPTER 9

CHAOS

I always thought I was content with the many blessings bestowed unto me. I've never been bored despite living for an eternity, there is *always* work to do. The universe has a never-ending supply of wounds to heal and tears to dry. What little of Evil it was exposed to so long ago still runs rampant, keeping me busy.

Nonetheless, I find when Cosmos leaves, there is an ache in my chest that wasn't there before. Contentment has fled from my forgotten solar system and only graces my presence when the young god returns.

It's quite frustrating.

Even now, as I lounge in my library's nook with a book in hand, instead of reading, I stare out the window waiting for *him* to visit.

I don't blame Cosmos for searching through space and time; one can never really rest until they've found their purpose. It's a longing that gnaws away at you, even when your life appears full.

I press the musty pages of *The Hitchhiker's Guide to the Galaxy* against my face and groan. "I must say, I hope he finds it soon."

"I've never read that one. What's he looking for?"

I nearly drop my book at Cosmos' cheerful voice and press the hardback to my thumping chest. "You *scared* me! I have a front door you know. No reason to just pop in."

I don't admit how excited I actually am to see him. I don't want to appear lonely. He'll visit me too often out of pity, which will keep him from what he's supposed to find.

"I thought we were past formalities," he says with a dashing grin, and moves to take a seat beside me. "May I see it?"

I bend my knees to make room and hand him the novel. "There are others, but this is the first one. It's an earthling series you may resonate with. It's about many things, but mainly, it's a story about a soul who searches for the meaning of life and their troubles in between."

"Hmmm," Cosmos hums as he flips through the old pages. "Do they find it?"

"Now, if I told you *that*—" I say and gently take the book from his hands, "—it would spoil all the fun."

He chuckles. "Even with made-up stories, there are no passes for me then? Just like a soul, it's essential I suffer while finding my own meaning? To be honest, after searching for a thousand years, it's become taxing."

I lean back into the nook and position my head to rest on my shoulder. From this angle I can admire all the stars decorating Cosmos's skin. *Ah*, I see now. He has a star for every year that passes. How brightly will he shine after he lives another thousand? The young god catches me staring. His gaze locks onto mine for a moment too long.

Uncomfortable with the heat rising toward my neck, I promptly stare out the window and make myself find the garden *very* interesting. Marta is in full bloom now. Her twilight leaves are decorated with baby pink flowers, their petals lined with a deep indigo that glows gently in the muggy darkness.

Cosmos pokes my right knee. "I know you want to say something. What wisdom do you have for a lowly, nobody god such as myself?"

I snort. "You're ridiculous. But because you *asked*, you should know that you have it easy."

He crosses his arms. "Alright, oh Great One. Enlighten me then."

"Well, you have it easy because you remember every search you've ever journeyed on. You also have an eternity to find your purpose. Unlike us, a soul inhabits a number of short lives, over and over again, never knowing what happened the last time, making the *same* mistakes, until *finally,* they find what they're looking for. Now how's *that* for insanity?"

Cosmos scoffs. "That sounds horrific. Now I feel bad for all those little souls wandering about. I'd never want to experience such a thing."

I chuckle, nudging him with my foot. "Me either."

CHAPTER 10

SLOW DOWN

"What's the rush?"

The woman behind the counter smiles shyly as she slides over my afternoon coffee. If she hadn't said anything, I would've missed the dimple in her left cheek and how her curls fall in just the right way down her shoulder. She tucks a strand behind her ear.

I'm caught off guard. Did she notice my impatience? I wasn't trying to be rude; I was just standing off to the side, waiting like always. Maybe it's my face? Feelings of awkwardness begin to set in as I pick up my order. My latte seems hotter than usual at my fingertips.

"You know what? I actually…don't know. I'm off a bit

early from work today and have nowhere to be. Maybe it's just habit? The hurriedness that is." Ironically, my last few words burst past my lips at the speed of an Olympic sprinter.

She shrugs and begins cleaning the espresso machine with a rag. "The daily grind does that to us. Maybe you should slow down? You're probably missing out on a lot."

Her sage advice makes me want to roll my eyes. I read the name *Sam* in block sticker letters on the tag pinned against her apron. The 'm' is slightly worn off.

"Okay then, *Sam*. Please do tell, what exactly could *I* be missing?"

By the way she peaks up behind the counter and searches about, I imagine the barista is on the tips of her toes. Sam is on the shorter side, as far as people go.

"Sorry, I had to make sure my manager isn't nearby. I don't want to get into trouble," she says.

My impatience rises. I wasn't expecting to have a conversation when I entered the café. I just wanted a latte.

Sam gestures to me with her chin. "Turn your cup around."

"Excuse me?"

"Just turn it around."

I shake my head but humor her. To my surprise,

there's a phone number hidden behind my index finger.

She puffs air into her left cheek and out of her mouth. "I've been scribbling my number on your coffee for *weeks*. But you never called. I thought maybe you just weren't interested, but then you didn't act any different either."

"I…didn't notice. Really, I didn't. I'm so sorry," I manage to stammer.

"Well?" Sam tosses the rag and puts a hand on her hip.

"Can I call—"

"I'm off at six. We can have dinner if you like?"

I beam from ear to ear. "I would like that very much."

"Good. It's a date. I've gotta get back to work, so…"

"Yeah, yeah, no. Go ahead." I wave her away, still smiling. She made my day. Maybe I *should* change my attitude? Slow down a little? Maybe I'd be less grumpy.

I reach the door and the bell jingles as I open it. Sam calls out to me.

"Hey."

I turn around, and there she is with my latte in hand. I didn't even realize I had set it down.

She offers me another grin. "Don't be in such a rush."

"DID YOU...

FALL IN LOVE...

TODAY?"

CHAPTER II

VULTURES

The vultures circle above my aching form, their tawny-brown feathers signaling that the end is drawing near. They can't wait to make a meal of what little flesh remains on my bones. Too bad for them, I have other plans. I've worked too hard and too long to be eaten by a flock of buzzards. When I die, I'm gonna go with a smile on my face and a bottle of whiskey in my hand. Right now, all I can think of is revenge, so I ain't fuckin' smilin' and I don't see no whiskey in this godless wasteland.

One overconfident vulture makes the grave error of swoopin' down. The scavenger gets a beak full of my jacket that's been patched over a dozen times. The conmen took my guns, but I never needed those. My fists do just fine.

I break the bird's neck.

I ain't *nobody's* prey.

CHAPTER 12

I AM A RACCOON

Despite the damp air, I am warm in my hollow. A shadow has fallen over the forest and the song of the feathered ones has gone blissfully silent in their slumber. Leftover sky water slides slowly off the leaves that belong to my tree. *Drip. Drip. Drip.* I do not like it.

All I know is hunger, and this want in my belly hastens me from my den. Though, it is difficult to wedge my girth out of the hole; I expanded recently and need to find a new home. Rough bark crumbles under my claws as I scurry across a swaying branch. Nourishment awaits me at the tip. The night is mine to feast upon.

There is a *snap*, followed by a *crack*, and then I am

airborne like the feathered ones. But instead of up, my jiggling fat takes me to the waiting ground. I do not like it. I do not like it.

I do not like it when I land in a nest of rotting leaves either. My thick fur bristles as I shake the hurt away. But it is not all bad—there is a buffet of small crawling creatures I now sit upon. They are quick, but I am quicker.

After my meal, there is thirst.

Mud squelches beneath the pads of my paws as I draw closer to running water. The journey to quench my aching throat is shorter than usual. The rock I like to sit on is nowhere to be found. By the time I catch danger's scent, it's too late. I'm swept away beneath punishing rapids. I do not like it. I do not like it.

I am spat out onto wet pebbles, half-submerged, drinking water I do not want. I do not like it, but I cannot move my girth. It does not listen to what I want anymore. I am scared. I do not like it.

I become airborne once more, but this time, my soggy fur takes me *up, up, up,* like the feathered ones. Water spills from my throat. Shortly after, I can move my body again. There is a rocking sensation, and I smell an unknown forest. Something gentle slides along my back repeatedly. It feels like a paw. From above, a song is sung that I do not understand. It is unlike the feathered ones.

I follow the sound and stare into a face that was made from the night sky. It is male, similar to the two-legged creatures who wander the forest in the bright hours.

The song is coming from the thing's mouth. It does not have fangs like me.

"Hey, *you*," it sings. "Don't scare me so much. You nearly drowned this time. I'll put you somewhere safe. You're not done here yet."

I don't understand the creature's song, but I *like* it.

"DID YOU...

FALL IN LOVE...

TODAY?"

CHAPTER 13

BASTARD

The three sisters hang high in the horizon, their heat scornful, though, with less intensity than my Taskmaster's disposition.

"Parry *left*, now," Josiah says with a bored sneer. He twirls an end of the monstrosity that graces his upper lip around a spindly finger.

"Parry left," I mouth facetiously, scrunching up my face to ensure I appear as horrendous as a spiked-heeled toad in the marshes. I do as he asks, though, and deflect my invisible opponent with the wooden practice weapon issued to me.

In my mind, I've laid waste to him a thousand times

on a gruesome battlefield. In these imaginations, Josiah almost bests me, but then I surprise him with a series of countermoves that makes him repent all the days he's spent mocking me. At the end, I shear that god-awful mustache off his face with gusto.

A chorus of steel-on-steel followed by grunts of effort echoes around me. I've yet to make it to the next stage in my training like the other novices. I'm being left behind *again.*

The Taskmaster puts his spider-like hand on my shoulder, leaning down and whispering into my ear, "You've shown little progress these past few weeks. I'd like to remind you, the only use for a bastard-child such as yourself is as a foot-soldier in the military, or as a wife."

Josiah squeezes *hard* with his fingers and I try my damndest not to wince.

"At this rate, you're not going to graduate with that shitty swordsmanship of yours. Keep making faces at me, and you'll find one day it may become stuck that way. At which time you'll have no purpose at all." Josiah shoves me and I land on the dry earth, skinning my knees and elbows in the process.

He places his boot on my practice sword and glares. "You see, no one wants an *unsightly* bride. So, when I say parry, you fucking parry like your life depends on it. Understand?"

"Yes, sir," I grind out between clenched teeth, choosing to swallow a retort that would earn me a punch to the gut.

He turns on his heel, showing me his back. "You're dismissed. Get out of my sight. When you return tomorrow, be prepared for the worst."

"Yes…sir," I say solemnly to the dust that blows over my calloused hands.

I'm an arrogant fool who knows what freedom tastes like—it's made me reckless. One would think being discovered as a bastard daughter of the emperor would make life easier, grand even. But it's just the opposite. My life is no longer my own. If I can't be married off or graduate from the academy, then I'm an embarrassment that has no function, no *purpose*. And it's a high crime and a hefty sum for embarrassing the emperor. My mother would know first-hand; she paid the penalty with her life.

Moister dampens my eyes as I scowl at the wooden sword laying in the dirt. *Life isn't fair.* I wipe away the tears and pick myself up along with my practice weapon. Maybe I'll create a world where it *can* be.

"DID YOU...

FALL IN LOVE...

TODAY?"

CHAPTER 14

CHAOS

As I peruse my playing cards dealt this round, I notice how Cosmos' gaze keeps flickering from his hand to the space behind me. I've bested him twice already; his mind isn't on the game at all.

"Something catch your eye? Has an intruder snuck in?" I'm careful to conceal my cards and shift in my seat for a better look, but there's nothing amiss nor interesting at the back of the parlor.

He shrugs and peers down at his cards. "No, nothing of the sort. I was just curious about the window behind you. I just realized its curtains are always closed, whereas all the other windows are uncovered."

Even though my forgotten realm lacks sunlight, the outdoors full of shadows, I still prefer the ambiance of an open window. But giving in to such a whim has caused me to error. Now, Cosmos' attention is drawn to where it shouldn't be. I try not to be too hard on myself. It was bound to happen eventually.

"That's because…there's no window there," I say, pursing my lips.

His dark brows lift in confusion. "Then why the curtain at all?"

I bend the corners of my cards back and debate how much I should tell him, or nothing at all. However, I've found in my long years that unanswered questions only breed more curiosity, and sometimes resentment. I don't mind how standoffish the other gods are, but I think it would hurt my heart a little if Cosmos became the same. Come to think of it, he *should* know. He's my dear friend, after all.

I play with the ends of my hair. "Well…the curtains cover the doors to Evil's chambers. Their appearance doesn't really go with my décor, and some of my guests have found them…off-putting?" Of course, when no one's visiting, I uncover Evil. I'm not entirely cruel.

The young god leans back in his seat. "Wait…what do you mean by 'Evil'? Is Evil even a 'who'?"

I rap my deck against the table perplexed. I thought I'd gone over this with him already? Maybe I wasn't clear?

"Cosmos, when I told you my purpose is to love the darkness, I was referring to Evil." I gesture with my chin to the covered double doors behind me. "That's where Evil lives. Why do you think the sun barely shines here, silly?"

My friend is a god who gleams with the brightness of a thousand stars, but the way he sits across from me, still and absolutely silent—well, if I were to put it into earthling terms, I would say that he's turned as pale as a ghost.

Finally, he speaks. "You're…married, then? To Evil?"

Winds of amusement build in my lungs, bursting from my mouth in a gust of laughter. He's so funny it hurts.

Cosmos throws his cards across the table and stands with such force that his chair topples over. *Oh dear*. He must think I'm laughing *at* him.

"Wait! Wait!" I gasp and try not to snort. "Don't jump to conclusions. I'm not *married* to Evil. One can't *marry* Evil. Evil is just Evil. Think of our living situation as a kind of guardianship. I'm their caretaker. The Almighty left Evil in my charge."

"Oh, well, then…" Cosmos glances at the mess he made. "I feel quite foolish now. You did tell me you had a relic in safe-keeping. Though, I would've never imagined *Evil* is what you meant."

"It's alright," I say, and help him pick up the scattered cards.

After we're finished, Cosmos rights the fallen chair. "I still don't understand. Evil just lives right *there*, beyond those curtains?"

I tap my chin. "Yes…and no? Technically a bit of Evil lives everywhere, but the majority lives inside the Chest of Pandora, which is where the doorway leads to."

"That's…a confusing explanation. Why do they have to live there, of all places?

I bite at my lower lip. I've never disclosed Evil's origins before to another. The story is complicated—nearly impossible to tell. I don't want to fumble it. Past guests quickly made their exit upon learning of Evil's existence; our conversations never went far. But here this young god stands before me ready for knowledge. What should I do?

"Well, if you don't want to say, I won't pry any further."

Anxiousness turns in my stomach. "No, no! I want to tell you properly, but do you mind if I put on a pot of tea first? It will help me think."

"Tea sounds just delightful." Cosmos moves to sit down, but then glances between the curtain, the table, and then back to me. "I have to say it. I'm coming with you to the kitchen. There's no way I'm being left alone in the same room as *Evil.* I can't do it. You can laugh and call me a chicken all you like."

A soft smile plays across my lips. I reach for him and give his hand a tug. "I would never. Come help me pick the herbs then."

He follows me, never letting go of my hand. A part of me is slightly embarrassed, the other is…happy. I'm used to everyone running away from me. Though I love Evil, being their keeper has its downfalls.

I move toward the kettle when we enter the kitchen, but Cosmos beats me to it. "Here, let me."

I almost argue—I'm particular about my tea—but, it's nice to have someone else make it for a change.

He's been here enough to know which cabinet holds what. When my friend deliberately skips over the plain set and chooses my favorite teacups instead, the gold heart in my chest jumps a little. He's been paying close attention to me.

Once the water is boiled and the leaves set to brewing, Cosmos carries the tray to the parlor and we take our seats. I tap my forearm with my index finger, suddenly nervous. "I've decided on the analogy I'll use, but it feels silly in comparison to the real thing."

"But why's a parallel needed in the first place?"

"Could you properly explain to someone how you were born from Venus and Mars without using a metaphor?"

Cosmos is silent for a beat as he sips his tea. "Point taken."

"Alright," I say, rubbing my hands together. "Now that's out of the way, I'll try to do my best here. When the Almighty breathed life into existence, it was kind of like a bland stew swirling about. There was life, but there was nothing *happening*. Time was born, and the Greatest of Gods thought life was rather dull with everyone always happy, always getting their way without a worry. Even after Death was born, everyone just piddled along without a care."

I hold up a finger. "So, the Almighty knew a drastic change was needed for this stew they created. And Cosmos, what do you do when a dish is bland?"

He sits straighter. "Um…add salt? Or spice, I think?"

"Exactly!" I wag my finger, "But, not too much. You don't want the spice to be overpowering, but also, you don't want there to be too little, because flavor *is* necessary. As such, the Almighty created the Chest of Pandora, and within it, Evil was born. Our Greatest of Gods opened this box just a hair, just enough to let a little bit of Evil out into the universe before they shut it for good."

I clap my hands together. "And that is the *very* edited version of Evil's origins and the Chest of Pandora. What an *amazing* tale, am I right?"

Silence as heavy as a planet weighs down upon us. *Oh my*. I thought I had done a good job explaining it.

Thunder rolls behind my friend's eyes. "Are you trying to be funny? Is this a joke? I've had quite enough of gods' horrendous humor."

Poor Cosmos, his wounds have yet to heal from what the others have done to him. Fortunately, I can reassure him.

"No, it's all true. I'll even show you their doorway. But fair warning, Evil isn't pretty to look at." I walk the ten or so paces to the curtains and fling them aside with bravado.

Cosmos spits up his tea and places the cup down with a shaking hand. "My gods! That's been *here* this entire time?"

I observe the double doors. Today, Evil has chosen the appearance of rotting human flesh, bruised and oozing. If I'm honest, I never know what's going to be behind the curtains. Evil makes it difficult to decorate, hence the drapery.

"These are just the doors to Evil's chambers. They're inside the Chest of Pandora, but they still have some reach, not too much though. This is as far as Evil can go."

Cosmos shakes his head. "Why do you have to keep the chest at all?"

"Well, *someone* has to. You can't just leave something like that floating around all willy-nilly into the universe. If the lid were to ever open, the results would be catastrophic. Other than the Almighty, I'm the only one with the capacity to love Evil." My chest puffs with a bit of pride. It's the one trait I inherited from my maker.

The worry in the young god's eyes turns curious. "Can I go inside and see this Pandora's box?"

"No, you cannot! The Almighty forbids it." I shut the curtains with unnecessary force. "I've already told you enough as is. But now you know all there is about Evil, and there is no reason to wonder about them anymore."

CHAPTER 15

REUNION

"Have you ever been out walking in the snow?" Amber's breath turns to vapor in front of her.

I blow air onto my naked hands, though it does little to help my frozen fingertips. I wasn't prepared for an impromptu adventure through the tundra. At least my jacket is warm, but the pockets on it are funny—a design flaw places the slits too far back. If I use them, I look like I'm impersonating a chicken. *Just my luck.* I should've known better than to shop in the clearance bin at the back of the Bargain Shack. I was also too cheap to buy gloves.

"Hell no." I grin at Amber. "I'm a Florida gal through and through. Give me a beach and some hot sun. Not—" I remove a hand from my armpit and gesture to the evergreens covered in winter's dust, "—*this*. I think you're crazy by the way for moving up here."

"It's cold, yeah, but I kind of like it. I needed something different." My best friend claps me on the back. "I've really missed you though, y'know? It's been so long since I've seen you. Thanks for making the trip." She stares off into the trees, her expression wistful.

Amber has changed since she left three years ago. I can't pinpoint exactly what it is, but she just seems like she's more somehow, more in a way that I'm lacking.

It's not necessarily bad, but we used to go bar-hopping together. We'd get into some kind of trouble before crawling back to our beds in the wee hours, just so we could do it all over again after our hangovers had worn off. Now we're hiking in the woods, a new favorite past time of hers. Like, who actually *likes* hiking? I thought that was just a lie you put on your dating profile to make you seem interesting.

I cross my arms again. "I'm sorry, I should've come sooner. You've already visited me twice." And that's the thing, I should've come before now, but I think I've been angry at her for moving in the first place. It's not easy when your other half just decides to go and leave you behind.

Three years has come and gone and it's like we're not each other's person anymore.

"Well, you're here now. When we get back to town, let's get you some gloves because otherwise, your fingers are gonna to turn into icicles. If I had known, we could've gotten them before." Amber elbows me playfully, "Were you trying to save a buck again? That's just like you."

My lips stretch into a wide smile. I've been found out.

She shakes her head. "Some things never change."

A gust of wind picks up and I squint against the cold while flurries of white snow stick to my clothes and hair. As the wind dies down, I notice how each flake of snow seems a little more beautiful when it's nestled onto the pinecones of the evergreens. The forest floor is transformed now that our tracks have been erased. Like a fresh start.

I turn to Amber, the hollow in my chest that's been present since she left not so empty anymore. "I think I may come to like winter after all."

"DID YOU...

FALL IN LOVE...

TODAY?"

CHAPTER 16

WHAT IS LONGING?

I'm in love. But my beloved is out of reach; she lives beyond my salted waters, up high in an uncharted realm without air. It would kill me to wrap myself around her glowing figure. Still, I never cease to wonder what that feeling would be like. The death would be sweet at least.

I've been told her name is *Moon.* That she is one of many in the universe, and my heart is silly for beating the way it does for her, that I'm an unrealistic romantic. The others can mock all they like; their laughter won't stop me from swimming to the surface to gaze upon her blurred image from my side of the waves. She shines best when pink shaded clouds surround her graceful form. I envy them, wishing I could be just as close, and closer still, in that dark indigo beyond.

I swim up as far as I dare, bathed in the halo of her light despite the rippling ocean that separates us.

My loneliness does not ease. She's there, but I am here. Pain blooms under my scales and I clutch my heart with webbed fingers. It hurts to be this far apart, to not even fully *see* her. If I could have just one clear look, *just one*, it would be enough to live on.

The frayed tether in me snaps, and I break the covenant that my kind, in their naiveté, made centuries ago—I cross the forbidden boundary.

Immediately, my gills and scales begin to burn in the open air, but I forget the sting because she is right *there,* and she is *beautiful.* In her full glory, my beloved is a luminescent pale gold. She wears a sky bathed in stars and stray clouds are wrapped around her full figure.

I ache to touch her, but though I try, my claw tipped fingers are *still* so far away. A strangled sob pushes past my lips. The burning intensifies, it consumes all that I am—the universe around me darkens. I have stayed too long in this place I was never meant for; the curse has finally reached my sight. This glimpse of my lovely Moon will be the last I'll ever see.

I let myself sink slowly below the waves. It is here in this eternal ocean gloom that I discover true longing. It's when you've been stretched thin, your insides time-worn, but the suffering is not enough, because if it were, my edges would reach *her*.

"DID YOU...

FALL IN LOVE...

TODAY?"

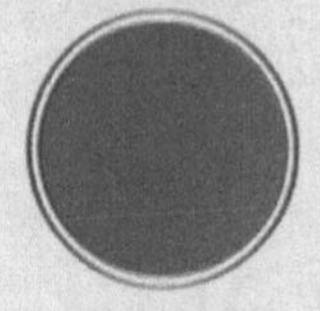

CHAPTER 17

BLEMISHES

As I follow the so-called fortune teller up the creaky stairs to her studio apartment, my prior doubts about the appointment return in full vengeance. I'm amazed at my own lunacy. I can't believe I let Nicki talk me into this. Sure, I've hit a rough patch—well, several, actually. That last stint at rehab did me some good, but I'm still a jagged mess. It's going to take more than a month to fix all my childhood trauma, not to mention the grand efforts I've made to fuck up my adult life. But never in my addiction-fueled dreams did I ever imagine myself seeking help from a…a…what the hell do I even call this lady? A witch? A whack-job nut?

I study the fine-boned woman as she fiddles with the

lock on the old door. She's dressed head to toe in flowing white cloth, even wears a matching turban on her head. And of *course,* her name is Circe. I wonder if it's a pseudonym or if her parents named her after the Greek enchantress. Either way, it's all crazy—but cynical me being here in the first place is even more so.

I imagine a future where I'm still alive and have children, or maybe even a niece or nephew. I gather the little tykes around me and warn them sternly, "Kids, don't do drugs, because if you do, the serrated bottom of it all will lead you to a mystic's run-down apartment and you'll give her your hard-earned money out of sheer desperation for her to tell you some bull-shit about life." *Ugh*, why am I also bitter in this version of myself?

Circe's buttery voice pulls me back to the here and now. "There! Finally got it. Thank you for your patience, sometimes the door has a bad day, just like us."

God help me. I'm going to *murder* my friend after this. "Hmmm…does it?" I almost ask if the door has big dramatic cries at night as well, but reserve my commentary.

The witch doctor disappears inside and begrudgingly, I take the last few steps to follow her.

I'm a bit surprised as I pass the threshold of the

studio. I was expecting something dark, or even garishly spooky, but it's just the opposite.

White oak floors are paired with fresh walls painted a creamy beige. The west side of the space has six tall windows overlooking a rare American Elm outside whose leaves have just begun to turn. Pots of Devil's Ivy and other plants hang from light-stained wood beams that run across the pitched ceiling. Matching shelves around the space are adorned with various crystals, books, glowing lamps, and candles. If I weren't a skeptic, I'd say this place is magical as fuck. Well, as magical as a hidden place on the Avenue can be in the great city of Baltimore.

"Here, make yourself comfortable." Circe extends a hand toward a sitting area with a seafoam blue couch, large beige ottoman table, and colorful rugs with floor pillows.

I've never been one to sit on the floor, preferring the standoffish dignity my metal folding chair in N.A. provides. But I don't see one of those handy and so instead, I take a seat on the couch.

In the process, I accidently rumple a throw blanket with constellations printed on it and do my best to smooth out any wrinkles. Even though this is all very grand, the ambiance of the space relaxed, my muscles start to tense up.

From therapy, I've learned it's all in my head, but even in the safest of places, it seems I always wait for a bomb to drop—the *gotcha* moment.

Like now, for instance. Circe places a gold lantern on the ottoman and lights a white candle within it. I try to convince myself this isn't strange at all. Plenty of people light candles during the middle of the day…in lanterns…don't they? *Shit.* What if witches are actually real? I swallow when she takes a seat on the opposite end of the couch.

Circe flashes a pearly smile and folds her long fingers in her lap. "I know Nicki sent you my way, but what really brought you?"

I jump a little in shock. "Are you really a psychic or something?"

She laughs and shakes her head. "No, no. Nicki *told* me she referred you after you made the appointment."

"*Oh*," I say and scratch my head, embarrassed. Of course that's what she meant. I'm really letting my anxiety get the best of me. Uncomfortable, I try and formulate a response as to why I'm here in the first place. My insides instinctively clam up, because how do I tell a stranger I'm at my end? That I don't think I can do *life* anymore? Whyever else would I agree to come here and see someone like her?

But Circe waits patiently at the edge of the couch, giving me all the time I need. A ray of light hits her face and shoulders at a certain angle that makes her appear angelic. It gives me courage.

"I'm just…lost? I guess? Every day is hard, and I don't know what to do. I don't even want to eat most days."

"Hmmm. Sounds like you're depressed," she says in a matter-of-fact way that pisses me off.

I snap at her. "Well, yeah! I'm a recovering addict and my doctor started me on these anti-depressants, but it doesn't fix everything! God, I can't believe I came here for this garbage." I stand to leave but Circe holds up a hand.

"Before you walk away, hear me out first. I already know what you think of me. I can see it in your eyes. You most likely came here as a last resort, but you might as well stay since you came all this way. I won't even charge for the time because it's not about that."

Damn, have I been that obvious? I don't deny it but shift a little as I sit back down. Well, if she's not charging, I guess I could see what she has to say.

Circe raises a brow. "You good?"

I clear my throat. "Yes...sorry for the, you know." I wave my hand about.

"It's alright. Thank you for the apology." She sighs. "I'm going to give you an analogy for your depression. It's not a substitute for science or medicine by any means, but think of it as an aspect of depression. What I'll talk about is the energy behind depression."

I want to laugh, but I've been rude enough as is. I wish I had popcorn for this.

The sage-like woman continues. "What if you thought of your depression as more like a pimple instead? And how does a pimple form? It's all this dirt and oil that's been festering in your pore, unseen, waiting to get out, until one day, the blemish appears."

"That's disgusting," I say and shift my elbow so that I'm leaning on the armrest. "But I'm interested."

"I know it is, but bear with me a bit longer. *So*, you've got all these hurt feelings that you're carrying around deep inside. Sometimes, you don't even know they're there, but regardless, your body doesn't *want* to be carrying all that ugly inside it. Well…it pushes it out eventually, like a pimple. These feelings manifest, and you become sad and lethargic until nothing matters."

I almost snort. Circe just described my last couple of decades perfectly.

She gestures to me. "What should you do when you get this way? What would *you* do if your depression were in fact, a pimple?"

"Um…I'd clean it, I guess? So, it would go away?" I shrug.

"Exactly! Now, *what if* you continue to follow your doctor's orders, keep taking your meds, *but*, at the same time, change the way you think about this disease that's affecting you? When your depression appears, instead of thinking, 'I'm sad or feel nothing at all today.' *What if*, you changed this thought pattern to, 'my body is getting rid of something it no longer wants and these feelings will disappear when they're cleaned."

I sit in silence for a few beats as I wrap my head around this logic. It's so fucking strange, but the most insane part, is that…it makes sense. If I were high right now, I'd say my mind is blown.

"But…"

Circe tilts her head, "yes?"

"How do I…clean it?"

"Energetically speaking, a salt scrub for your bath or shower, and cutting all the chords these hurt feelings stem from. To clean your energy, you must do this every day, with intent, until the depression stops. And *again*, when it resurfaces."

I'm dumbfounded by this conversation. I don't entirely understand what she's saying, and while I still think Circe is a kook, I don't necessarily think she's lying either. But here's a fact I do know— I'm buying some damn salt on my way home today.

CHAPTER 18

A SPURIOUS CHILD

Nervous, I gnaw on my lower lip as I make my way through the overgrown woods of the mountain. I'm exhausted after walkin' for hours on end, but night will fall soon and I've yet tuh find proper shelter. Every knotted tree and encroachin' shadow is sinister under the settin' sun. I rub my salt crusted eyes with the back of my hand, my cheeks are swollen and warm from all the cryin' I've done.

I'm still in shock, the reality of my banishment not quite settled on my bones just yet. The townsfolk have always treated me strangely, sure, but I never expected Maw and Pa tuh turn their backs and side with em'. I thought they at least loved me a lil', well, Maw did anyway. Pa always had a hateful temper.

I hiss when a long-twisted branch claws at my bruised back. My neighbors threw stones, some findin' their mark as they screamed, "Be gon now yuh changelin' git!"

"Changelin'?" I mutter tuh myself. "They've all gone mad." This foul business with witches, fairies, and now changelins has gotten out of hand. I'm not the first innocent tuh be ran out and won't be the last. At least they didn't go and drown me like poor Sara. How the bloody hell was tha' sposed tuh work out anyhow? The blameless sink and the guilty float? Either way, the girl turned out just plain bloody dead.

"It's insanity is what it is," I huff, heart racin' from the steep incline. There's a part of me tha' knows this is for the best. I was bound tuh leave tha' tiny patch o' land anyhow, with a drunk pa always thinkin' I'm some spurious child, no good came of my bein' there. I've gotten plenty of heavy licks from him in my life—enough tuh learn tuh be quick on my feet.

Legs burnin', I grit my teeth. "I'll survive just fine without em'." My only sorrow is tha' I left my lil' Abby behind. There's no one else tuh take care of her. I think she'll grow in tuh a fine mouser, though, and get by. Still, I'll miss tha' warm purr of hers.

It's nearly pitch black now with only the waxin' crescent-moon and the stars tuh guide me. I could be more wary about creatures of the night, but I'm damn tired and the moss off the path looks like it's just as good as any place tuh lay my head. I make tuh set a new course, but my boot slips on a rock and then I'm tumblin' down the mountain at a bone-breakin' speed. First, it's my left arm tha' snaps, next, my knee. I'm impaled through the shoulder and become an embodiment of tear-blindin' pain in my continued decent.

Strange paintins' fill my head and I know I'm experiencin' death as I fall—my simple life appears before my eyes. But amongst those torn paintins', there are others; they're me, but not me. In the many, there's a demon creature with a fin, a girl with a knight's sword, and should I dare say it? A raccoon? I've been a bloody *racoon*? At this point, I know the insides of my head must be mashed and tha' God is grantin' me the kindness of a delusion tuh ease the hurt.

Finally, my body rolls tuh a stop. It twitches, slick with blood, and the gory crimson drips into my eyes from my damaged skull. Maybe it's best it turned out this way, I never wanted tuh live a life alone anyhow. But as my sight fades, twin creatures appear above me. The two possess enlarged eyes and their wings glow like the moon. I laugh at my insanity, but it comes out wet and red spews from my mouth.

"Is it broken?" the one on the left asks with a voice tha's been crafted from a small bell.

The other creature shakes its head. "Not an 'it,' you fool, are you blind? He's one of ours. See, *there*, his mask is starting to fall."

The twin chimes, "Ah! Shall we fix him then? His birth mother would surely want him back." It scratches a long ear, its flesh the color of lavender. "Though, she should've sent for him by now, he's nearly that age."

"Who knows, but enough chit chat! We best get to work before he bleeds out. What a mess this is."

Under the twinklin' stars and the lush canopy of the woods, their little hands go tuh work, makin' what was once broken whole again. Despite this wonder, all I can think about is how my bloody Pa was right all along.

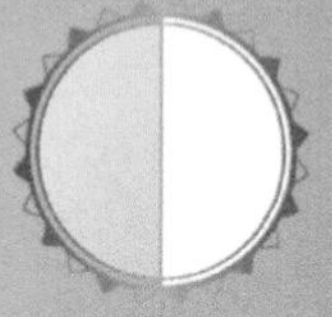

CHAPTER 19

PARALYZED

Eyelids closing, you hear a faint hum.

It grows until it's deafening.

The persistent whir, a battering ram against the insides of your skull.

Your fingers twitch as your REM cycle is disrupted.

Without warning, flames appear.

The fire caresses your body,

devouring the air in your lungs.

You can't escape—you're paralyzed.

You're certain the world is ending.

Beyond the flames,

within the shadows,

the Devil looms.

He looms.

He looms.

He looms.

But he's just there to watch.

To consume your fear.

Your terror makes him stronger.

You can't help but feed him.

You know it's the Devil, because you continuously make excuses not to go to church. God's holy ground makes you squirm. You loathe it. On Saturdays you plot your escape, because every Sunday, your grandmother requests your attendance at church. The morning of, you tell your tired mother that you're sick. Sometimes, you even go as far as to steal the thermometer from the medicine cabinet. You vigilantly place the instrument against the lightbulb of the lamp until it reaches the perfect number of 102°F.

Most of the time you win, and triumphantly saunter back to bed until your mother forgets that you're ill. When you lose, when your mother has lost all patience, and just wants to be rid of the burden of her troublesome daughter—you find yourself stuck in a pew singing the Lord's gospel. Your grandmother smiles happily though with a red hymnal clutched in her withered hands. Foiled gold letters that read *The Holy Spirit,* glare at you from the cover.

You think of this as you're wrapped in flames. You know you're being punished for all the times you cursed God while sitting in Sunday school. The Devil has come to collect your soul, and even though life has been cruel—you beg for him to go away. You scream with everything you have. You try to move, to thrash wildly, but your limbs are frozen. You don't understand this vision of the world ending or why you're the one who must witness it.

Miraculously, the humming stops.

You find yourself on top the antique bed, buried within *The Little Mermaid* sheets you share with your younger sister. Your heart is racing because you realize the Devil is real and that you should've been praying all along. Trembling, you glance at the digital clock on the nightstand—it reads 3:00 A.M., the witching hour.

The wind howls outside, and you worry a deadly storm is coming. Spring isn't kind to Oklahoma. The collision of hot and cold brings tempestuous gusts that make even the sturdiest of buildings fall. You peek over the rumpled blanket and stare out the window—your father forgot to close the curtains when he tucked you in. Through the glass, a tree's branches whip back and forth, scratching the pane like an arachnid monster. You cower, fearing the Devil will come again if you close your eyes.

You roll over and face your sister instead. Her round angelic face is caught in sleep and her crown of dark curls cascades over Sebastian's crustacean legs. You're envious of her peaceful oblivion but scared as well. You reach for her shoulder and shake it.

You whisper, "Play *Mario Kart* with me."

She blinks groggily but doesn't complain at being woken up.

Soon you are both racing along the Rainbow Bridge. The faint glow of the box television highlights the faces of the porcelain dolls your mother forces you to keep in the corner. You stare back at them as they watch you—they make your skin crawl. In the game, you hit a banana and your kart spins out of control because you weren't paying attention. Your sister laughs, but she doesn't see how the controller shakes in your hand.

The squeal of rusted hinges makes you jump—the door just opened.

"What are ya'll doin' up!" your father barks. He's angry because you have school the next day and he caught you awake past your bedtime.

You tell him that you're scared of the dark, but he doesn't believe you.

When you're forced back to bed, he threatens to take away the *Nintendo 64.* He thinks you're crying over the console, but he doesn't know you barely escaped getting your soul stolen only moments ago.

Your sister falls back asleep quickly, and you watch the popcorn ceiling above. The cracks stretch wide like canyon gulfs—as does your fear. You look for a distraction, anything to keep you from sleep, to evade the beast that waits in the confines of your closet.

You notice loose threads on the sheets. You pick at the frayed strings of Ariel's hair, and count how many stiches you unravel. Time stretches, and you know you'll be safe if you last until sunrise.

But you're little and begin to lose track of the red fibers. Your fingers slow their movement as your eyelids become heavy. You twitch when the humming begins anew. Flames dance around your bed and you watch as civilization crumbles. Your gaze travels to the open space beside you and finds the Devil standing there. He was waiting all this time.

"DID YOU...

FALL IN LOVE...

TODAY?"

CHAPTER 20

CHAOS

I'm watering Marta when anxiety suddenly blooms in my lower abdomen. I pause to touch my stomach, marveling at the oddity. I'm an ancient goddess, I don't get such feelings. Something's amiss, but what?

In a flash, the unrest grows, snaking upward until danger's vine has my heart completely ensnared. The watering can slips from my paralyzed fingers and lands on the ground with an ominous *thump*. A ringing starts in my ears until all I can hear is the damned noise.

My bare feet become soaked. In the invisible chaos, I wonder where Cosmos is. I note how he's taking an unusual amount of time in the kitchen. The young god wanted to have afternoon tea in the garden today, and he insisted on brewing it himself.

The ache crawls up my throat, choking me. My eyes widen from the discomfort, and a single tear escapes down my cheek. Is this the call of Evil? Has something happened to them? With grand effort, I manage to snap my fingers, leaving the garden to reappear inside the parlor.

I'm greeted by eerie subterfuge. Deceit's wicked kiss has my knees buckling beneath me, my golden heart seized by panic's vice grip. Evil's double doors are wide open. They've taken on the appearance of ordinary wooden doors, but Cosmos's tortured screams from beyond their threshold tell a more sinister story.

"*No. No. No. No. No*!" I gasp as I crawl forward. It's as if there are hundreds of needles stabbing at my skin, a sure reprimand for neglecting my guardianship duties, but this punishment is light in comparison to the one dealt for trespassing into Evil's realm. Despite the pain, I manage to get to my feet and run.

When I enter Evil's chambers, my house fades away into a realm of blood and swarming flies. In the distance, a beam of light placed long ago by the Almighty burns bright. The buzzing insects attempt to blind my path forward, but I know my way and swat them aside. Crimson sludge oozes from a black sky, coating my hair and arms—I choke on the putrid stench of it. Beneath my soles, the wet ground pulsates, assuring me Evil is angry for being disturbed.

Why would Cosmos come here of all places? He wasn't *made* for it. His screams have turned into dull moans that echo across the blood river. I'm almost out of time.

Lungs on fire, I near the ray of light shining down on Pandora's Chest. My insides crumble at the sight. The simple black box sits undisturbed on a dais made of bleeding stone, but at its feet, Cosmos lays dying—his stars burning out, one by one. Evil's curse eats away at him, turning his body back into dust. Only the young god's upper half remains.

I hurry to bridge the gap between us, falling to my knees at his side. "You fool!" I chide. "Why would you do this? I told you it's forbidden for anyone else to tread here."

Cosmos reaches for my hand and squeezes it. "I just wanted…to see the one…you love so very much. It was silly of me, wasn't it?" He chuckles sadly.

I can now taste his jealousy on my tongue, a flavor most bitter. I should've detected it sooner, this part of *Evil* that lives inside him. How was I blind to such envy? And why would he be jealous of Evil? I shake my head; it doesn't matter.

I gently caress the last beautiful star on Cosmos' knuckle with my thumb. "Evil has placed a curse on you. I can sense them through your hand. You're returning to dust because you've not existed long enough to endure it." I purse my lips as I bite the inside of my cheek. "You're not even old enough to bargain your way out with magic."

Cosmos winces. "Lady Fortune has never once smiled my way, and she certainly wouldn't show her teeth to me now. Chaos, this Evil is painful. I don't see how you tolerate them, let alone *love* them. You're a marvel in every way."

The thought of Cosmos not existing anymore is too much. I can't stand to see his brilliance dimmed before my very eyes. At this point, it's really not such a hard decision to make. He's my dear friend after all. "I'll take the curse for you, I'm well old enough to bear it. I'm as old as Death, nearly as old as Time, after all. Let's see what Evil's bargain is about."

"No! You can't!" Cosmos tries to jerk his hand away, but his strength is no match for mine.

Closing my eyes, I open myself up to the curse which deafens me to his protests. Evil floods my being, they're a rush of painful love that's been twisted to the blackest shade of darkness. Within it, I sense their bitterness toward my friendship with Cosmos. They despise how close we've become and wish to punish me for it.

"*Youuu do not really looove meee,*" Evil whispers. "*This entire tiiime, you've been lyyying. You're nothing but a fraaaud.*"

I try to soothe them. "You and I both know that's not true. I was made to accept you, to love you, just as the Almighty does. There's not a thing about you I would change." A pitiful aspect of Evil, is that all they've ever wanted is love. It's why they commit such horrendous acts, so desperate they are for affection.

The darkness hisses at me, "*Then prooove it.*"

I sigh. There's no point in quarreling with Evil. They've always possessed a child-like stubbornness and will forever continue to be the way they've always been. "What would you like in exchange for the young god's life then? I'll bear his punishment for disturbing you."

I feel Evil's smug pleasure through our bond. "*In retuuurn for the thooousand stars I'm looosing to your meddling, you Chaos, will provide meee with a thooousand short liiives in their place. You will become a looowly soul, and within at least one of your liiives, you must fall in looove with meee.*"

My lashes flutter in surprise. That's not such a bad bargain—the time will pass as quickly as light travels. I'll be back at my house, tending to Marta and having tea with Cosmos in no time at all. But like with any curse to ever exist in the history of the universe, there is always a catch. "And what will happen if I don't manage to love you in one of these lifetimes?"

"You will ceeease to exiiist. Even the duuust you leave in your waaake will fade to nothiiing. This will beee your ultimate punishment for lyyying to meee since myyy conception."

I tilt my head in thought. Loving Evil *is* my purpose after all. How hard can it be to fall in love with them? "It's a bargain," I say. "Now that you've had your fill of terrible fun, return those bright stars back to the young god, please."

Time has never been a precious commodity to me, but as I watch Cosmos' eyes widen and his mouth stretch into a horrified shout, I wish above all else that I was given a moment to say a proper farewell. But Evil is Evil, and their wickedness waits for no one. My holy godhood shatters into a tiny, fractured soul. Following the breaking, a tidal wave of sadness crashes upon my existence. It's ironic. In all the time I've spent loving Evil, not once, has Evil ever loved me. In fact, no one has. Only my great Maker.

CHAPTER 21

WASTED TIME

A rare golden feather descends from a sky cast in hues of angry gray. It brushes past my nose, grazing my upper lip, its edges, soft as silk. The scent of summer lingers where the feather touched—which is absurd, because summer, along with the other more pleasant seasons, ceased to exist a long time ago. Now, only gray remains.

Some call it the Endless Winter, but harsh as that season was, winter at least made you feel cold, made you feel *something*. I would know, because I lived it. I'm one of the few remaining who has—I'm a breathing relic. What we've been left with is a storm without rain, without *purpose*. The livid sky withholds precious water. Forever in a tantrum, it shouts and booms only to remind the last of us, that we are indeed damned.

Thunder rumbles, and I wonder what kind of bird would fly in this kind of squall, but then again, maybe an angel simply lost their way. As if possessed, I follow the feather's whimsical path through the wasteland. I know it's illogical, that I'm most likely seeing ghosts in my old age. Birds are extinct and the angels left us to fend for ourselves when we broke our sacred vows. Still, a light of hope exists within me. *Maybe* not all is lost. *Maybe* they've returned to us. *Maybe* we're forgiven.

I reach out with veined fingers; however, the gold rarity eludes me—like it's teasing. I've lived a time-stretched life, and a part of me knows I should be grateful, but there is an agonized half that begs to know why I couldn't have disappeared with the others. What was the point of wandering about with the world's final vagrants? It's been a waste of breath, a cosmic joke with no punchline.

I'm close to a chasm carved deeply into the land by one of God's punishing knives when my spotted hand finally grabs hold of the feather. Its golden silk quickly crumples under the pressure of my fist. I *ruined* it.

The abyss on the other side of the precipice smiles,

welcoming me with open arms in a way that God never did. As I stare at that gaping dark, the past thirty years of hunger, thirst, and loneliness lash out with all their rage. Why did I have to *live* this way?

.

.

.

But God doesn't answer, nor do the angels.

.

.

.

I'm *done* with this *farce*. I step forward with the crushed golden feather still in hand. The descent is long. Wind whips past as I plummet, and my consciousness starts to fade in and out from the pressure change. During the fall, there is a whisper I strain to hear. Am I hallucinating? The voice is familiar to these old bones, even though, I've never heard such a handsome sound. To my dismay, he's angry, desperate even.

"YOU LEARNED

NOTHING

THIS TIME."

CHAPTER 22

;

Today my insides twist like strangled roots of a tree. There's just no more air, it seems. I woke up this way. I *woke up* this way. Now, how's *that* for living?

"DID YOU...

FALL IN LOVE...

TODAY?"

CHAPTER 23

BAKED BEANS

On my walk home from school, I count to seven on my fingers and wonder how I can become unstuck. Because that's what I am—stuck. Seven more years is a long time to be a child. I want out of this arrangment *life* forced onto me. My father tells me I was an accident, but no one bothered to ask *me* if I wanted to be born in the first place. If life were a person, I'd call her an inconsiderate [enter expletive].

My science teacher asked me not to cuss as much, and because good ole Mrs. Jackie teaches me about the universe and how we're all just a hodgepodge of elements on a giant rock—I decided I would at least try. Still, I love the way "*bitch*" sounds on the tongue.

Sorry Mrs. Jackie.

It's my eleventh birthday and there won't be well wishes, candles, or cake at home, but I do have a can of baked beans I nicked from the lunchroom waiting for me in my backpack. I don't even like baked beans. They're gross and slimy. Beans shouldn't be sweet, either—that's just wrong, plain and simple. I don't know why they exist, much like myself. But someone in this world *loves* them. Someone literally thought, I'm going to create *this*, and now, here they are.

Just like me.

At least, that's what Mrs. Jackie says. She tells me every day that I'm special, that God loves me and thought me into existence. God never asked what I wanted, but I guess that's okay. Because regardless, I'm *here*, and I'm gonna make the best of it.

CHAPTER 24

A CONVERSATION WITH MY PHYSICIAN

I treat every tomorrow as if it were a plague to be avoided. Popping open a can of Red Bull at 8 P.M. so I can stare at my phone with bloodshot eyes into the wee hours under gnarled sheets. It's my fool's attempt to delay the inevitable. Sometimes, I look up from whatever distraction I've conjured and plead for the sun on the other side of my bedroom curtains not to rise.

10:46 P.M....

12:20 A.M....

1:52 A.M....

It's 3:08 A.M. by the time I find my way out of

whatever vortex I fell into. I've learned this habit of mine has a name, a *diagnosis*—Revenge Bedtime Procrastination.

What genius came up with that moniker? Who the hell am I getting revenge on by stumbling down an internet rabbit hole while the moon is out? I'm certainly not smiting the billion-dollar industry whose profits I pay homage to everyday with my time and sanity. Because even if I stumble in tired, with freshly painted dark circles under my eyes, I'm still punching that office clock punctual as ever.

I chuckled when I was prescribed the term. I pictured a villainous me, rubbing my hands together, plotting how I'll overthrow the next day-to-day routine with another Netflix special. "MUAHAHAHA," my imaginary self said maniacally in his boxers on the couch. *Stranger Things* is going to be the downfall of my tyrant boss. Maybe he'll be warped into another dimension entirely. Huzzah!

In this fantasy, I of course had a long mustache that curled just so.

I never once viewed this time as a negative. Just the opposite—I find my nightly adventures a peaceful respite. Everyone else in the house is asleep, no one wants anything, no one is complaining, I can just be *me*. These short hours are a relieved sigh from the strangled breaths I hold all day. But now, I'm being told that I'm *mental*, that I have a *sickness*, and that my beloved cure is *sleep*.

....

"Come again, Doc?" I say and wag a meaty finger at the bloke dressed in his long white coat. I've got some thoughts that need to be voiced. I tell him with a hint of defiance, "Maybe *I'm* not the sick one. Maybe it's the *earth* who's ill."

"Mmmhmm…I see." The doctor swivels his chair toward the monitor of his computer. "Well, I'll get your script sent right over to the pharmacy. We'll have you back to sleeping in no time," he chimes happily as he types gibberish onto the keyboard.

I flip him the finger behind his back. What a *wanker*.

"DID YOU...

FALL IN LOVE...

TODAY?"

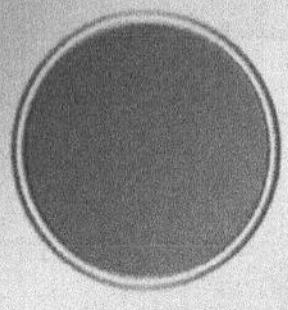

CHAPTER 25

RAGE

What is the difference between those who release all their wrath and those who remain calm when they're angry? I'd like to know this superpower, this *magic*, the calm harness. Right about now, I'd kill for it.

My nails dig into my palms under the pressure of a heavy fist, scraping skin—but it's my knuckles that sting, my heart who took the hit. Her cheek already swells red. By tomorrow, a bruise will linger to remind me of my sins. She's a mirror to reflect the monster in me.

"I'M SO SORRY."

"SORRY."

"Sorr…"

"Sor…"

"So…"

"S…"

…

And I *mean* it, with every ounce of my being, how *sorry* I am. Sorry I exist at all. Sorry she's unfortunate enough to ever have met me. I don't know why I'm this way, why I can't contain this rage in me, this inferno that wants to burn the world down. The excuses I've given her are as empty as a desert lake, but even still, she accepts them like rain to our drought.

The cruelest part is that I *let* her forgive me. Let this thing we've become continue breathing for the both of us.

We *need* help.

"I don't deserve it. I don't deserve *you*," I tell her.

"I *know*," she says softly, and kisses my guilty knuckles.

"DID YOU...

FALL IN LOVE...

TODAY?"

CHAPTER 26

COSMOS

Through the centuries, I've asked Chaos this question over and over in hopes her curse has finally broken, but she never hears me, never really *sees* me. Thanks to her bargain with Evil, the other gods' jest about my invisibility came to fruition. Though, it's only her eyes I no longer exist in—the only eyes that matter. Despite my question falling on deaf ears, I'll continue to ask Chaos every day, until she finally falls in love with the one she's *supposed* to love.

I bite down on my tongue as I watch her walk hand in hand with another on this warm summer evening. Even the ocean pines for her as I do. Its dark blue waters reach for Chaos, washing away the sandy footprints she leaves behind.

I imagine it's out of jealousy, but this blinding envy is all in my head.

She's taken on many forms over the years, each of which I've loved. In this life, her bright tresses remind me of a sun's rosy hues at dawn, her skin the color of porcelain dusted with pink. There are constellations perfectly placed across her face that cascade like falling stars down to the tips of her toes. I've learned these maps of small worlds written onto humans are called "freckles." I've also learned that Chaos hates them, hates her body, even hates the name she was given. I wish I could take all this hate from her and crush it to oblivion. She should never have to feel such ill-repute about herself.

"Divinely beautiful." A whisper only the wind will hear while I watch her from afar. This is the true meaning of *Astrid*, the name her birth mother bestowed unto her this time. If she only knew how fitting it truly is for a goddess such as herself.

Chaos' human companion pulls her close, wrapping their arms around her waist before they kiss her tenderly—kiss her how she deserves to be kissed. In this way, she is happy. A small consolation for the suffering she must endure on my behalf. I'm eternally grateful to this lover of hers, and the previous ones, as well as the lovers she'll meet in the future—but even my hallowed gratitude has its limits. I turn my gaze the other way, this envious heart of mine can only take so much—a terrible sentiment I share with Evil.

Chaos wasn't the only one cursed that cruel moment when I witnessed her divinity shatter into a thousand different colors like a broken kaleidoscope. To not to be by her side in the ways I once was is pure misery. It's even more so to watch the goddess I adore be deeply in love with so many others. It's as if she's the sun and I the moon—we're always in the same sky, but never really touching.

I rue the day in the garden when I first began to care for my friend. In doing so, I caught Evil's wicked eye. It would've been better for Chaos if I hadn't let such affections into my heart. Evil's jealousy knows no bounds and they're an absolute glutton, never tiring of this peculiar dish of revenge they've cooked up. For how *dare* I, Cosmos, fall in love with a goddess the Almighty created distinctly for Evil?

It's ironic that someone who burns so bright was made to love the darkest of monsters. I can detect Evil's terrible mirth for my situation from beyond the threshold of their double doors. I've been connected to them since the bargain was struck and stand guard in Chaos' place until she can return—that is, when I'm not checking on her soul's progress. In the time I've picked up her guardian duties, I've determined that if my heart were ever the size of the entire universe, there is not a corner of it, not a shred of it, not a molecule of my being, that could ever—*ever*, grow to love Evil. In fact, if I could find a way to wipe their scourge from the corners of every world, I'd destroy them without hesitation.

On the coattails of that horrible thought, I sigh and cradle my face in my hands. Loneliness has made me a hateful creature and if I were ever to abolish Evil, it would leave Chaos without a purpose. I could never do that to her. I've already hurt my beloved goddess enough. But I'm awful still, because I'm frightful of every day that passes her by. I'm an immortal god in every way, but Time is my enemy. The magnitude of her purpose is a sizeable burden to realize, and doubts of her ability to do so creep in more than I'd like to admit. I worry she'll live a thousand lives and never fall in love with Evil.

A shooting star passes me by in the indigo sky and I wish on it fervently with all the hope I possess. I wish for Chaos to rediscover her purpose, for a day when I can finally convey my feelings to her. If it comes true, I'll tell her how I fell in love with her when she was just Chaos, and then again, during all these lifetimes where she's been a burning flame only to be snuffed out.

Her lifeform known as *Astrid* takes a seat on the sand below and rests her head against her companion's shoulder. They point to the same shooting star and make a wish while the waves crash gently against the beach. She puts a hand over her belly and one of her glorious smiles, as bright as a hundred suns, plays across her lips to light up the darkness within me.

It's this very moment I fall in love with Chaos *again,* for the umpteenth time. In the gentlest of ways as she lives this ordinary human life of hers. And *again*, in this passing second where she laughs at something silly her partner says. And *again*, as she gets up to dance in the full glow of the moon.

My silver heart breaks before it pieces itself back together with the threads of her happiness. I tell her words that will never reach her ears, a whisper only the wind can hear. "Chaos, I have fallen in love *again*, for the umpteenth time, with *you*."

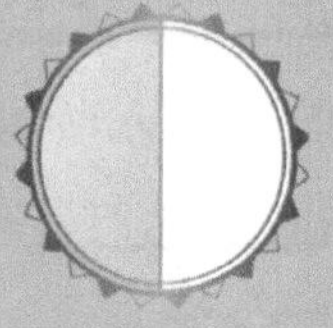

CHAPTER 27

A BAD TRIP

I'm sitting at a bar, the kind of bar that used to be a neighborhood drinking hole before a forward-thinking hipster decided to come along and fuck everything up with their new money. The bitter locals keep coming though, because it's an easy enough walk from home to wet their beaks. They sip on their same beloved beer and cocktails; the only differences are the five-dollar upcharge and the dehydrated fruit that decorates their glass. But what the hell do I know? I'm on vacation, without a care, and my brain is breaking from the drug I took.

My body knows I should've only taken half of what my friend slipped me, but my ego didn't know any better.

The molecules of my DNA go wild as they start to expand, my cells bouncing around in an excited frenzy for what's to come. It reminds me of the cartoon, *Osmosis Jones*—because all these little parts of me really *do* talk to one another. The thought makes me snort.

Next to me, Alec finishes his IPA. He raises a dark eyebrow and his voice against the surrounding bar banter. "You, okay?"

I don't possess the rigid control I usually have. The muscles around my mouth move of their own accord, which now pull my lips into an insane smile. "Uh huh."

He shakes his head and orders another drink from the bartender, and so do I, even though the Old Fashioned in front of me remains untouched. I down it, knowing I'm getting too old for this. The mixture of bourbon, bitters, and cherry burns the back of my throat.

Our bartender is attractive, maybe in her mid-twenties with long braids that reach well past her shoulders. She slides Alec's beer over to him, the foam spilling just past the rim from her over-pour. As she gets to work muddling the sugar cube of my cocktail, everything slows, and I realize my brain can pause the outside world like a TV show I've grown bored of. People become frozen puppets around me.

What.

The.

Fuck.

Simultaneously, this is both terrifying and wonderful. It makes me question my sanity. Is *anything* real? Fuuuuuck…Now, inside my head, I'm warping through time.

My consciousness travels to a future where I walk away without paying my tab. This pisses off the pretty bartender who presently stands motionless across from me. It then warps to the past where Alec ordered us pub food and made a cheap pass at the woman next to him. She politely turned him down with a strained smile.

I fast-forward from that moment until I'm at the time I need to be in. The bar comes to life once more like I just pressed play. My shaky fingers fumble for my wallet, and I struggle to pull my credit card free. Somehow, I manage, and slide the plastic toward the bar's edge.

"I need you to run this now, otherwise it won't get paid," I tell the bartender as she hands me another Old Fashioned I probably shouldn't drink.

I don't think she heard me properly because she simply taps the Visa against the wood, and says, "Sure thing,

I'll pre-auth it."

She sashays away and Alec leans in close so he's next to my ear. "Are you sure you're alright?"

I deadpan, "My brain is put-put-puttering out." Because it is. The gears of my brain are turning and stopping and turning and stopping. It's a strange sensation, to be aware that you're malfunctioning but can't do a damn thing about it.

"*What*?"

The gears shudder like a machine that needs oil and I know that what I'm about to say will make me appear unhinged, but you can't stop a calamity if it's supposed to happen. "I've been warping through time. It's weird, like, I can *pause* everything when I want to."

My friend snorts. "You're *tripping*, drink some water."

Alec took the same thing I did, but he doesn't seem to be ripping the fabric of time and space. Just me.

Our food arrives and I struggle to eat as nausea rises in my abdomen. I press pause on the outside world and warp through time. I see myself puking all over the bar. *Oof*, I don't want *that* to happen. I travel again, to an alternate timeline and see myself hugging the toilet inside the messy bar bathroom. *Gross*. I don't like that either. I come back to the present and know if I don't leave now, that one of these two situations will occur.

I stand up and gather my belongings. "I gotta go, I'll meet you back at the Air B&B. Take your time."

"Um…Okay?" Alec says around a mouth full of food. "Do you want me to box your plate? You only ate, like, a chip."

"No… No food." I feel guilty for ruining the evening, but things are about to get bad. I hurry outside to the crisp October air. Miraculously, I don't puke.

I make it back to the room. I don't remember the particulars of walking here, or grabbing my luggage from our rental parked outside, or carrying it up two flights of stairs. But I find myself up against the bathroom wall next to a porcelain goddess with her lid wide open. My brain has indeed broken, the gears completely off their axels, because there are hundreds of voices in my head, all fighting for a chance to speak.

What in the hell is happening to me? I hand over the microphone that is my mouth. I can't fight them off any longer. *They* answer my question. "It's like the movie *Split* and *Inside Out*." These words move past *my* lips, with *my* voice, but they are not *mine*.

Fuck.

Fuck.

Fuck.

I do *not* like this. I have zero control of my body.

"We're here all the time, even when you don't realize it. Helping you," they say with my mouth.

Alec appears in the bathroom doorway. "Dude, who the fuck are you talking to?"

I wish he wasn't such a good friend to follow me back, but rather one of those shitty ones that would've taken advantage and stayed out. At this point I'm like a spectator watching a horror show. A very fucked-up horror show.

"Seriously, are you okay? You left the bar in a hurry."

I want to answer, but *they* still have the microphone. "His mind is breaking, the body should've only taken half," they say to Alec with my voice.

I'm embarrassed as I watch the whole thing unfold and wish it would stop, but it doesn't. He kneels slowly in front of me. My legs begin to twitch. I can't help it.

"Fuuuck, you are on one bad trip, bro."

He needs to call the police. Shit, I would if I were him. I can't stop this train wreck from happening. "Did you knowwwwww, when we remember, we're actually warping through time? That thoughts are an expansion of timmmme?"

Alec shakes his head. "You've been saying that shit over and over since we ordered our drinks."

"But its truuuuuue. The brain doesn't want to remember this tomorrow, so don't tell him."

"God you're so weird." My friend stands and disappears from the bathroom.

Spectator-me wants to die. Spectator-me hopes none of this is really happening. The ones with the microphone assure me this is no illusion though. That this is *supposed* to happen, and there is no warping my way out of such event.

Alec returns and sits in front of me, legs crossed. "Here, eat this. It will make you feel better." He places half of a chocolate bar in my hand.

A childish version of me smashes it up like it's mud and giggles. "It really is just like *Split*, you know," they say into the microphone. But they aren't talking to Alec anymore, they're talking to me. "How do you think they got the idea for all these movies? It's time that everyone knew about the *We*."

My friend jumps to his feet. "God, bro! Throw that in the toilet and get the fuck to bed, you're starting to freak me out."

Spectator-me vows to never do drugs again, of any kind. I warp through time and see me hating myself tomorrow.

"This body should've only had half," they say.

Alec still thinks they're talking to him and pulls me to my feet. "Dude, thoroughly noted. Next time you're getting a quarter. A FUCKING QUARTER. Now go the fuck to sleep."

He dumps me onto the nearest couch in the living room, and I close my eyes against the humiliation of letting him see me like this. I don't sleep through the night. Instead, my consciousness travels beyond the veil of illusion to other dimensions with other versions of myself.

They tell me the purpose of suffering, and how everyone is part of the *One*. How we're intricately woven, yet separate fibers who have chosen their part to play on the grand stage that is the universe. When dawn arrives, I want to lock the knowledge away inside a box and never open it again. Because if nothing is truly real, then what's the point of it all?

CHAPTER 28

THE SONG

Deep within the woods, I don a mask painted in vivid colors of a twilight sky—my favorite color, my favored time of sky. For it's neither dark, nor is it truly light, yet the sun and moon come together for a vibrant performance.

My brother and sisters dance around a tall flame. That hungry light crackles and hisses alongside the night's song. Soon, it will be my turn to join them, but I am nervous to do so. My fingertips brush against the guise I chose, and I wonder if it is the right one.

Before it was my time, a brother told me a story, sang me a future I am terrified of. From this night forward, I will wear a mask each day, and play a role. Like the sun, like the moon, I will put on a performance of my choosing.

In this dance, there will be mountains crafted from strife I must forge a path through, but I should not despair, because moments of joy will find me on the way. All this trouble I must endure to search for my heart's song that has escaped my chest when I wasn't paying attention. I must catch it and hold onto it until I fall. I asked my brother what the point of this journey is, why we must put on these acts, for in the end, the song is always caught.

He sang to me, "It's how we learn to love one another. How we learn what happiness is."

I asked him then if this song and dance are worthwhile, but he wouldn't answer.

As the flame before me rises higher and higher, reaching for stars it can never have, my brothers and sisters dance ever faster. I swallow my fear and join them. It is time to find my song.

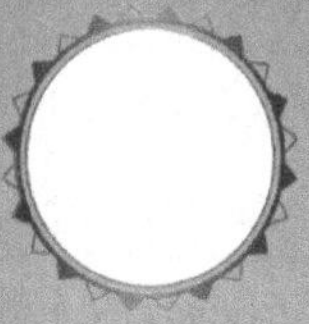

CHAPTER 29

GROWING PAINS

I must love drowning because I keep doing it. Not just metaphorically, but literally. I sink to the bottom of the pool, my lungs shouting at me to hurry the hell up and do something. But I can't; *I don't want to.* My limbs know this and refuse to propel me upward to a surface that doesn't want me, that *rejects* me. I just want to sink and sink and sink until I black out and my brain finally dies.

But alas, a strong grip encircles my boney arm and yanks me back to reality. Death doesn't come so quickly for those who wish for it.

Over the noise of shouting children, the lifeguard yells, "Make room! Make room!" He sits me down on the warm concrete and starts with chest compressions before he presses his lips against mine. He tastes like strawberry Chapstick, his sharp cheekbones smeared with coconut sunscreen. A familiar feeling stirs under my swim trunks. I force my brain to think of kittens, of big fat manatees, of my annoying next-door neighbor with her ugly Chinese Crested dog. Nausea surges and *it* goes back down. I throw up the chlorine-filled contents of my stomach, barely missing the lifeguard.

God, how I hate me.

Keith pats me on the back. "You okay, buddy? Did you forget to take your insulin again? Do you want me to call your mom?"

I wipe the leftover vomit onto the back of my hand. I'm not even diabetic, but it was the quickest excuse I could come up with when I nearly drowned the first time at the neighborhood pool. I'm fifteen and should be able to swim by now. It's embarrassing.

"I'm fine. No need to call her. I left my medicine at home, so I'm gonna go now."

Keith, a junior in college who's home again for the summer, places a concerned hand on my shoulder. "You want me to get someone to walk there?"

At his touch, I start to think of manatees again, but the Chinese Crested seems to do the trick. I shrug him off and get to my feet. "No. I only live a block or two away. I'll make it."

He calls after me. "Are you sure?"

I grab my towel from nearby and slip my feet into the black Nike slides my dad bought me, the ones I hate. "Yeah, don't mind me."

As I close the pool gate latch, I watch Keith's girlfriend saunter over to him and hook a graceful arm around his muscled bicep. She wears a white bikini over the peaks and valleys of her body and says something I can't decipher; she's probably oohing and ahhing over her boyfriend's heroics.

Jealousy stirs within my heart, but not at their relationship. Men are a dime a dozen, myself included. I touch my chest, noting its flatness and how my arm is more bone than skin. My parents are starting to worry because I don't eat enough, and when they aren't watching, I throw up my meals. I can't stand the thought of my body changing, of growing muscle, of becoming *masculine*. The mere thought of it makes me sick. My voice has already betrayed me, it's no longer a tenor, but an alto. I've adopted the habit of not speaking unless I must. I can't change this body I was born into, and so, I do the only thing I can—I wait for it to die.

My sliders scratch against the concrete while I make the short trek home, the hot summer sun already makes me sweat. A street over, someone mows their lawn. The buzz of their machine lulls me into a place of imagination. A different world, where I have a body that curves and bends, like a winding, scenic road. In this world, I am content, I am happy, and I am enough.

The sound of a grating metal pulls me back to reality and I look to my right to see Do-hee, who lives three houses down opening the lid to her garbage can. In the crook of her arm, she holds a withered houseplant, the ivy leaves brittle and dry.

She catches my stare and smiles sadly, nudging her dead plant in my direction. "My poor hedera died."

I don't know why I bother or care to ask, but I do. "What happened to it?"

Do-hee sighs. "I know what she looks like now, but it's not that I didn't water her enough. I know that much. What happened is that she outgrew her pot. With hederas, if you don't change their pot in time, they quickly die."

"Well, that's… sad," I say.

She shrugs. "It happens." My neighbor throws the dead plant into the bin before replacing the lid. "Have a great day," she says, waving at me, and goes back to her house.

I watch after her until she closes the door behind her and think about the hedera left to rot inside her garbage can. It doesn't sit right with me, so I quickly open the lid and reach for the ivy that now lays askew atop the garbage bag.

On my way home, I hold the plant against my damp chest, its dark soil smearing over my skin. At its base, a single bright leaf remains alive and well. Do-hee must've overlooked it by mistake. She's like my parents. Adults don't see a lot of things.

I whisper to the growing hedera, "Little girl, you just need you a new pot is all. I'll make you good as new."

Like this plant here, I'm not done growing yet. But we differ in one way, because I'm done letting this pot I've been shoved into strangle me. I'm going to live, I'm going to thrive, but most of all, I'm going to be *me*.

"DID YOU...

FALL IN LOVE...

TODAY?"

CHAPTER 30

NIGHT WIND

Woken from yet another nightmare, I sit on the steps of my family's front porch with my legs tucked against my chest. A lukewarm mug of chamomile tea rests on top of my knees. I cradle the ceramic between clenched fingers. My heart aches with the fear of failure as I watch the night wind whip the leaves of a towering oak in our yard. The generational farmhouse at my back creaks with each powerful gust.

Every cloud is in the sky, it seems; they cover the moon, the stars, and their light. I've been having vivid dreams lately, in these disturbed patterns, a darkness whispers for only my ears to hear.

It says to me, "You will not succeed."

The words are a seductive pull to despair, to self-pity and loathing. I want to push these stifling feelings away, stamp them down until they are nothing but floating particles, never to be seen or heard from again.

But I've come to realize that's not how fear works. Because fear will always rise again, no matter how many times I brandish a weapon against it or grind it down to dust. I know now that it's a part of me, engrained into my being on a cellular level. And if I'm ever to become more than what I am, how can I truly do so, if I cannot understand and accept this dark thing inside me?

My thumb slowly glides over the rim of my mug, and I stare into its contents, the teabag floating atop the untouched golden liquid. "It's admirable, actually," I murmur to myself. That is, the way fear rises, over and over again. If fear can manage to get up after being defeated so many times, then why can't I?

CHAPTER 31

ARE YOU LISTENING?

"Only One Guest at a Time Please," reads the new sign posted in the cramped entryway of the groomer's colonial building. I blow warm air up onto my sweaty face. It's too damn hot to stand outside.

With a sigh, I clutch a squirming Coco to my chest and take a stance against the wall opposite to the glass door. I wait for the woman on the other side to finish her business at the register, the white poodle at her side wags its curly tail.

As I stare out at nothing, I notice how the powder-blue floral wallpaper has begun to peel near a corner of the crown molding. There's also a crack in the ceiling. I hold Coco just a bit closer, suddenly anxious. This happens from time to time—absolutely nothing has occurred, yet I'm still anxious about the *nothing*. Maybe I should go see a therapist—or a doctor. Maybe they have a magic gear that would fix the frozen clock inside me.

The bell above the glass door jingles as the woman exits with her poodle, but there isn't enough space for all of us to fit. I immediately apologize for my existence and try to become one with the peeling wall. The "sorry" that comes out of my mouth is something I've been conditioned to do. Coco kisses my cheek with her pink tongue.

"Don't apologize," the woman says firmly to me, face stern. She brushes past with her happy poodle in tow.

It's only a second, a speck of sand leaving life's hourglass, but as I watch her go, I think I'm hallucinating because I hear something, almost like music. And there's a shift—a *tick, tick, tick,* as the clock in my chest finally begins to move.

I step into the groomer's small lobby with a sense of wonder and new purpose. Just now, I think I had an encounter with an angel, their ethereal song now implanted deep within my marrow. It goes like this: "Your existence is not a mistake. Don't erase your footsteps."

And I *hear* it. God, do I hear it.

CHAPTER 32

A WRITER'S DREAM

I'm groggy, my body pumped full of what must be morphine. I struggle with the simple task of opening my eyes. The *beep, beep, beep* of a machine registers before the stale hospital room does. Above me, the florescent lighting is a shock to the system.

I pull the putrid green blanket that's been draped over my emaciated form up to shield myself. In the distance, a telephone rings incessantly. Why won't anyone answer it?

"Mom? Are you awake?"

Under the blessed cover, I blink and I struggle to remember that I have a son. A good one at that. He's given me excellent care since I was diagnosed late last year. It's been bliss seeing my grandchildren every day.

"Seems like it," I tell him. "What am I doing here? You know how I feel about hospitals."

There's a sigh, followed by a shuffling of footsteps before I detect Will's strong hand at my shoulder.

"You fell *again*. You've been in and out of it for… three days now." My son's voice wavers on the last part. He's been more upset about the cancer than I have, even talked me out of signing a DNR. But I won't apologize for being eighty-four years old and dying. Death catches up with us all at some point. It's just how the story of life goes.

Still, I lower the blanket and give his hand a gentle pat. "You're going to be okay without me."

Will's brown eyes are watery, and I know he's giving his all to keep everything bottled up.

I pinch the skin of his thumb. "Quit that nonsense. If you feel like crying, you go and have a big cry. If you want to scream, do it at the top of your lungs. No point in holding everything in like some sleepy volcano. That shit's poison for your heart."

He cradles his face with his other hand and gives a hearty chuckle, a white smile flashing between his fingers. "I'll try to remember that."

"Be sure you do, that's a gold nugget of wisdom I just gave out." In an attempt to get warm, I nestle myself further into the blankets; hospitals are always so damn cold. In the process, my eyes land on the brightest corner of the room. It's filled with an abundance of flowers, baskets with chocolate, cards, and other trinkets.

"They're from your publisher as well as some of your fans. There's more where that came from at the house." Will must've saw the slow gears in my brain puttering about.

"Really?" It's been nearly five years since I had any work published. I decided to retire and just write solely for me when the Muses visit. "I thought they would've forgotten me by now."

My son walks over toward the shiny hoard and starts picking out some of the cards. "Far from it. You've even had some local fans try and stop by for a visit. They were a bit put out when we turned them away."

I don't know what to think about this. I've always been a private person. I'm not sure how they would've known the cancer bug bit me. Will hands me several cards, the seals broken on each of the envelopes.

"I didn't read them; I just know how you hate opening your mail."

Like a good son, he remembered. A smile stretches my dry lips and I reach for him with frail arms. "Give me a hug. In all my accomplishments, I know my greatest of all was you." It's probably not the most original comment, but writers can use idioms if we want, especially in this case, when it's true.

He does as I ask and wraps me in the warmest embrace, planting a kiss on my withered cheek. "I love you, Mom," Will whispers. "Now, you read these while I call for your nurse. The doctor will want to know you're awake.

"Ugh!" I tell him and cross my arms like a petulant child.

He laughs. I really hate hospitals and all the poking and prodding from the staff. But as Will walks out the door, I know it's the last time I'll see him. I only woke up to say goodbye. I'm not sad about it. I've had a long life, one filled to the brim. I'm truly lucky that I even had this final moment with him.

I stare at the spread of envelopes on my lap. I know my second greatest accomplishment was this. Some of them simply say how much they love my work, but it's the ones who tell me they felt something, had an experience when they read my words, that I know all the suffering in my life was worth it.

I have my critics, for sure. Those who say my writing is painfully dreary, or that it's grotesque "depression porn." But my words aren't for the carpers—they're for the people who felt like they were being punched in the gut while reading them. My sad prose is for those who suffered how I suffered—for the ones who need an outlet for their heavy, gruesome feelings. And as I sit here and read a young woman's letter, my hands tremble from its effect. *She felt seen.*

I lay back onto my blankets and pillow, my chest rattling with its final breaths. I think about the phenomenon of life—how every little moment in mine mattered, each leading to the next. As if something, or *someone*, plotted out this great map specially for me. And how I couldn't have had all my happy times without the sad ones. Those events that left deep jagged scars are what *made* me. Without them, I would've never started writing, and I would've never been able to make such deep connections with others. I would've never met my son's father. And for *that*, I must thank the villains of my life and their treachery.

In truth, after all this time, I can now say, I even *love* them a little for it.

"YOU...YOU...

FELL IN *LOVE*...

TODAY?"

CHAPTER 33

CHAOS

"You... You… fell in *love* today?"

The familiar voice I haven't heard in over ten millennia is a like a forgotten song to the ears—cozy, yet beautiful.

Cosmos' gaze is filled with wonder as he stares at me from across the parlor. He sits alone at the table with a pot of tea, his back to Evil's covered doors. The young god stands in a rush, knocking over his teacup, spilling steamy liquid everywhere.

My knees start to shake, and I have to steady myself against the wall. All my memories encompassing the span of a thousand short lives, rush me at once. The experience is dizzying. Though some were brief and some much longer than others, all my adventures were impactful.

Tears crest at my newly-restored eyes. I was in a daze when Death took my withered hand at the hospital. The old god was in such a hurry to get me back home—they were probably worried the Almighty would send me back for another go at it. I don't want to think poorly of the deity, but based on their attitude, I'd say Death is just about sick of me.

"Are you alright?" Cosmos reaches for my shoulder, his touch reverent.

"Of course," I say, and wipe away a pesky escaped tear. "It's so nice to *see* you again. I missed you even when parts of me didn't know to miss you."

As the young god stands before me, I note Cosmos' brilliance is tenfold. Only a fool wouldn't see him now—he shines with the radiance of a hundred thousand stars. I hope all the other gods are envious when they gaze upon him.

"I… I…" Cosmos stammers, his hand trembling on my shoulder.

Concern for his wellbeing pools at my belly. I hope he made friends while I was gone all this time; otherwise, he must've been incredibly lonely. "Now it's my turn to ask. Are *you*, alright? I know I cut it close, waited until the last life to relearn my purpose, but I —"

Without warning, my dear friend wraps his star-dusted arms around me in a crushing embrace. His chest heaves as he sobs into my hair. "It was all so hard, and I'm so sorry you had to endure a soul's pain, just so an envious monster like me wouldn't disappear."

I return his hug while he continues to cry—it feels nice to be held in his arms. "You deserve to be and to exist. I would do it all over again, I would even live a thousand more lives if need—" Cosmos puts a hand over my mouth, silencing me.

"Don't utter such a thing, Evil is listening—" he gestures toward the covered double doors behind us, before giving me a defiant stare that makes my chest flutter like the wings of angels, "—and I would rather die the true death than let you have a soul's experience ever again. I know it was you who lived, but it was excruciating for me to watch from afar."

I remove his hand and give us some distance before my heart flies away entirely. "You shouldn't concern yourself anymore with Evil. You've done well enough guarding them in my stead. They're a sore loser, but can recognize when they've been beat."

My friend palms his face in obvious exasperation. "I don't think you're quite understanding me."

I'm at a loss for words. What did Evil do that would frustrate Cosmos so? They must've been tormenting him in my absence. I glare at their curtains, they're no doubt rotten behind them. Someday we'll have a little chat about all this, but not right now. "How about we get some air and away from Evil for a bit?"

Cosmos gives me a gentle smile. "That would be wonderful."

We take a silent walk out to the garden, where I notice how Marta has been well cared-for and is even ready to bloom. Slow as gravity, I finally digest what Cosmos said earlier and stop my stroll immediately. He bumps into me.

"Oh, sorry," he stammers.

I whirl on him. "What did you mean when you said you watched me from afar?"

All of Cosmos' stars light up like a band of supernovas and I have to shield my eyes until he stops blushing. He really gets embarrassed far too easily.

"I… I… watched over you, just in case there was a way I could help somehow. And I did help when I was able to intervene. The whole situation was my fault, after all."

I nod, specifically remembering a time when I was a raccoon, as well as some other brief cameos he made. Heat rises up my neck. Now it's my turn to feel embarrassed. I made some silly mistakes that he may have witnessed. "How many lives…did you see?"

"All of them."

"All *thousand*?" I gasp. "You watched over me for ten millennia? Weren't you bored?"

He turns his face to the starry sky. "I just wanted to wait for you is all… It's not like I was stalking you."

That's *exactly* what he was doing, though I don't say so. "But why did you do it? Why did you wait so long for me? Did Evil drive you insane? Is that it?"

His jaw clenches, and as I gaze into the depths of all he is, I realize that somewhere along my journey, Cosmos lost his youthful gleam. It's been replaced with a wisdom that even surpasses some of the elder gods.

With a firm hand, he tilts my chin up and stares directly into my eyes. "It's because I *love you.* I will always love you. Even when all the galaxies fade, and their suns die, the constellations will remake themselves, and signal to the universe that *you,* Chaos—are my beloved."

I'm stunned by his confession, and in a daze still, as Cosmos graces my lips with a tender kiss that I eagerly return. He tastes like windy summer nights and dreams, and the kind of longing that aches and aches and aches. Our kiss turns passionate, and I realize, I've been waiting the span of my entire life for this moment, for *him*.

I'm trembling when it's over, dizzy even, as my lonesome planet spins on its axis to become an entirely new one. Cosmos shines with the brightness of a hundred thousand stars and this time, I cannot look away.

"Do you understand now?" he asks.

I caress his cheek. "I do. I'm sorry it took a few ages."

Cosmos tilts his head to kiss the curve of my palm. "That's alright. We've got eternity to make up for it."

Smiling, I take his hand, and we walk together amongst the stars of space. I'm almost as old as Time, as old as Death. I was *made* to love the sins of others, to love the darkness, to love *Evil*. But I never thought, nor could I ever have imagined, that someone, *someone*, in this expansive universe, was made to love *me*.

Thank you for reading!

Time is not linear, and neither is Chaos' story. For more of her short lives, please see: @athousandshortlives on Instagram.

For additional books and art by W.B. Clark, visit: *wbclarkbooks.com*

Future Adult Titles:

Giving Up Elysium

Heart of Áïdes

For Children:

So, You Want to Be a Witch?

ABOUT THE AUTHOR

W.B. Clark is from small-town Oklahoma, mostly raised on a farm full of chickens and then partially on a boat in Alaska. She graduated from the University of Oklahoma (boomer sooner!), then moved to some big cities, where life happened. She finally got a job that pays her bills, and sometimes, she gets to write books and illustrate pretty pictures on the side. In between, she plays random instruments poorly, swears often, and wonders where her next adventure will be. Some of which involve hiking, camping, scuba diving, and starting complex projects she knows little to nothing about. She loves coffee, wine, cigars, her husband, and their beloved one-eyed shih tzu, Minnie.